THE
JEWEL MAKER

Books by the same author

Fiction

APPRENTICE
JOURNEYMAN
SURVIVOR

Stage Plays

REVIVAL!
BE YOUR AGE
SCHELLENBRACK
THE ONLY STREET
BRIGHT SCENE FADING
THE PAROLE OF DON JUAN
MR JOYCE IS LEAVING PARIS
OUR KINDNESS TO FIVE PERSONS

The
Jewel Maker

Tom Gallacher

HAMISH HAMILTON LIMITED

First published in Great Britain 1986
by Hamish Hamilton Ltd
Garden House 57-59 Long Acre London WC2E 9JZ

British Library Cataloguing in Publication Data

Gallacher, Tom
  The jewel maker.
  I. Title
  823'.914[F]   PR6057.A388

  ISBN 0-241-11866-2

Phototypeset by Eagle Graphics (Phototypesetting) Ltd,
Ilkley
Printed in Great Britain by
St Edmundsbury Press, Bury St Edmunds, Suffolk

To the memory of Karen Blixen, for whom there was, and is, always another story to tell

Contents

The Jewel Maker

The obsession seized Martin Doyle with an urgency which was bewildering for his family and his girl. When he collapsed at Dublin's main bus station a friend brought him back, not to the girl (whom he'd left) but to his mother's old house. He lay there all day, speechless, immobile and staring at nothing. Late at night he gratefully fell asleep and in the morning his brother Richard came to see him. Thereafter, those most closely affected by the crisis kept a day-long watch with Martin. He knew – and they came to realise – that *that* day was all the time there would be.

They tried to arrest his departure by making an obstacle course of the past and bringing into play the combined forces of threats, love and cunning. Their assault began, rather surreptitiously, while Martin was still asleep.

Before Richard and his mother went upstairs she told him he must try and force the lock on the large canvas holdall which Martin was carrying when he was found. Mrs Doyle, called Beatrice or Beattie by all who knew her, was a compact woman in her mid-fifties, careless or just slovenly in appearance, and practically a chain-smoker. Her normal mode of address was loud and dogmatic. It was only with some effort that she managed to lower her voice to a volume notionally unlikely to wake the sleeping figure on the bed. She pointed to the corner of the room, 'There! That's his bag. There's a lock on the end of the zip.'

But Richard went first to look at his brother. Not much could be seen. Just the top of his head and a few long straggly locks of blond hair and the edge of a bruise on his right temple. The breathing was regular enough, though. 'He's dead to the world.'

Beatrice, kneeling on the floor, was already sliding the bag into a more accessible position. 'Shhh! Let him sleep.'

'I've never been able to rouse him on purpose,' Richard said. He was wearing his working clothes, including his heavy ridge-soled boots, and he crossed the floor with exaggerated caution.

'Can you force that?' his mother asked.

'Why don't we take the bag down to the kitchen?'

'And him wakin' to find it gone?' Beattie demanded in a whisper. 'He'd think we were pryin', or stealin' on him.'

'We *are* pryin'.' Richard inserted the slimmer of the two blades of his pocket knife under the catch of the small padlock. 'There!' The hasp attached to the bag zip sprang out. Beatrice immediately opened the bag and started delving through the contents. Richard caught her arm and stopped her. 'Here, let me. They're his private things.'

'What private things can he have from his mother?'

'Things. I'll do it.'

Beatrice hauled herself to her feet with the aid of Richard's shoulder and fetched a chair on which the unpacked clothes could be laid. Richard took the opportunity of her distracted attention to remove a tightly tied bundle of correspondence from the corner of the bag. He glanced at the handwriting and address on the topmost envelope and quickly slipped the packet inside his shirt. With his back to his mother he said, 'I wouldn't let you search through my stuff.'

'Your stuff was spread all over the house. There was no call to search. Didn't I trip over it?'

'What are we looking for?'

'Some explanation, that's what. Some reason. A letter maybe.'

'I'll not go near his letters; nor will you.'

'And suppose he's never able to rise again, or speak again? How will we know the cause of it?'

'He'll be all right.'

Beatrice again got down on her knees. 'He's far from all right or I wouldn't have got you here before your work.

He collapsed in the street and he's speechless. Where was he goin'? That's what I'd like to know. There must be a ticket, or an address in there. I've looked in his pockets.'

'Of course ya have.'

'Ach!' She cuffed the back of his head. 'All I found was somebody's business card.'

'Maybe he was goin' for a real job at last and the thought of it overpowered him.'

'I doubt it.'

'And what good can it do if we…'

'Shhh!' Beatrice threw a sharp glance over her shoulder at the figure on the bed. He hadn't stirred.

Her older son, more softly, asked, 'And what good am *I* to do – apart from forcin' the lock, which you've had practice in yourself.'

'What good? Oh, that's a rich one! That's a rich casual question to ask *me*.'

'Well?' Richard insisted.

'Your only brother is sick of God knows what ailment … and I tell you of it, and you ask me why?'

'What good can I do if the doctor says he's just to rest?'

'It would take a powerful doctor to set my mind at ease; with him like that. Lost and childish again.'

'Have you told Kate?'

'You're sure there's no address – or warrant, maybe?'

'Warrant! God help us, no.' Richard completed the task of replacing the clothing in Martin's bag and carefully pulled the zip to its full extent. He tried to reinsert the end into the lock but it wouldn't go and hung loose over the end of the bag. He helped his mother to her feet. 'Have you told Kate he's here?'

'Isn't it Kate he's left?'

'She should be told. He's been living with her for…'

'That's enough!'

'I'm goin' to tell her. I'll go by there on my way.'

'He's well apart from her.'

'He's not well. That's why he's here.'

'He's here because Felix brought him here in his car; thinkin' Martin was drunk.'

Richard protested. 'But Martin doesn't get drunk.'

His mother sniffed. 'Felix refuses to believe that of

3

anybody.' Reaching into the torn pocket of her wrap-around apron for her cigarettes she led the way out of the room and when Richard joined her on the narrow landing she carefully closed the door. 'Well, that's that. And we're no further forward. Not a sign. Lucky it was a friend saw him, for he carries no way of tellin' who he is.'

As she descended the stair she let her voice resume its normal hectoring volume. 'If the hospital had got hold of him they'd say he was a missing person – or think his was the name on the card.' She paused at the foot of the stair and fished the card out of her pocket. 'D'ya know who that is?'

'I don't know any of his friends now.'

'Friends don't give you visitin' cards,' Beatrice asserted and shuffled in her broken-backed slippers into the kitchen.

'What did you do with my bed?' Richard asked abruptly.

'I burned the headboards and kept the mattress. It's in the loft.'

'But you kept everythin' else the same.'

'I've had no choice.' She banged the frying pan down on the hob, then, haphazardly, started assembling the food for Martin's breakfast. 'If I had a husband or a handy son, it would have been re-decorated long since.'

'Is the doctor coming back?'

'He said he'd look in during the day. And look in is all they do for what they're paid.'

'You're glad Martin's back, aren't you? For whatever reason.'

'Away to your work.'

'Everything exactly as it was before I left school.' Richard went out into the weed-infested back yard under thin spring sunshine. He called back. 'Why did you burn the headboards?'

'For warmth,' Beatrice shouted and shooed him off.

Richard picked his way over the broken flagstones of the side path towards his car. The house was the last one of a decaying terrace of workers' cottages. A wash-house had been added against the gable wall. Its tarred sloping roof was just below the window of the bedroom in which

4

Martin lay. Glancing up, Richard recalled the pungent smell of tar which had enveloped them at night after those long, burning hot days they'd spent in school. Martin had remarked on that. 'All we get of summer is the smell of it.' The tarred felt was split and ragged now. Indeed, many of the houses on the terrace had been condemned, as had much of the surrounding area which was once a thriving bustle of small factories and large busy warehouses feeding the canal wharves.

The house was in the Kilmainham area in the south-west of the city close to the old harbour of the Grand Canal. The place stank of decay and could not have provided more of a contrast to where Richard now lived. His home was a modern bungalow in Killiney, with space and trees all around and fresh air off the sea. For a moment, as he stared at the car parked by his mother's gate, it was difficult to believe the vehicle was his. The only cars that had ever stopped there were the Garda patrols in the middle of the night, while he and Martin upstairs in bed had buried their heads under pillows to muffle the sound of the law looking for their father, and Beatrice at the door protesting. It was a sickening, frightening feeling, for they knew that next morning they would have to walk down that street with all the other children on the way to school. They would have to face the jeers of the children; and the patronising sympathy of the grown-ups who knew whose sons they were. The children were cruel and their elders did nothing to stop the cruelty.

'I'll never forget walkin' that street,' Richard told me. 'There was only Martin and m'self. It seemed the whole world was just Martin and me and the only street was that one, with nowhere to hide.'

'"The only street",' I repeated. 'I've read that in a poem.'

Richard grunted. 'Well, *I* didn't read it in a poem, let me tell ya. I walked it – time and time again.'

Nevertheless, when I came to write a play about Martin Doyle and his obsession, that was the title I used: *The Only Street*. And by then I'd tracked the quotation to a poem by Emily Dickinson. For the actual substance of the play I had to rely on the participants in the action and my own reconstruction based on what they told me. And that still seems the best way to report the events.

Richard now drove through the narrow streets, which seemed much broader with so much of their boundaries demolished. He also recalled how his mother had to cadge food on tick and how far she had to walk to reach shops where she wasn't known. The fear and the hunger and the inability to change their lives had affected both brothers and for a long time it seemed they, together with Beatrice, were a single cell of some resistance movement which could not possibly achieve victory. Thinking of Martin's present condition, Richard guessed the strain and tension of their youth was now affecting his brother as it had once affected him. As he changed gear and headed up Steevens' Lane to cross the river, he pressed his fist against the bundle of letters he'd concealed under his shirt.

But Richard *had* achieved a kind of victory. He was a steel erector. When he told people this, he always had to explain it was nothing to do with putting up tubular scaffolding. That would greatly underestimate his wages, skill and value. His job was piecing together and connecting, at a great height, the ribs and vertical structures which form the skeletons of tower blocks and other high-rise buildings. They were not structures normally associated with Dublin, but they were on the increase now that Eire had discovered how to milk the EEC development fund. American investors, too, always wanted new buildings and tended to think not only big but tall. Richard was highly paid for danger.

In the small bedroom of the brick-built terrace house Martin was waking up. At least he was allowing his body to show signs of the waking that he himself had been aware of for some time. He'd dimly heard the conversation between Richard and his mother but had not responded to it because, frankly, he could not believe it

6

was really taking place. There was something else: the inhibition, too, of the very frightening memory of his limbs refusing to move while he sweated with the effort of imposing his will upon them. Even his tongue had lain heavy in the bottom of his mouth while he frantically expelled breath over it to form words. He'd produced only the sound of gasping breath.

Now that he could, he rolled over and saw that he was in a place where his mother and brother might well have been talking. He wished he had paid more attention to what they had said. He lay on his back, breathed deeply and extended his arms before clasping his hands behind his head. With surprise he noted that he was wearing an unfamiliar shirt. A faded, greenish shirt which was much too large for him. He made a quick exploration under the bedclothes and discovered that the shirt was all he was wearing.

The movement had disturbed the bedsprings. Even if he'd been struck blind that sound would have assured him he was at home. He rocked a few times more, as though playing an ancient harp he'd never expected to hear again.

As the faint sunlight edged around the building and laid a pale stripe on the far wall, he became acutely conscious of the room. He sat up and beamed with delight. His expression suggested that the cramped, shabby room was an annex to wonderland in which, with great good fortune, he had been most carefully deposited. The smile on his face went on smiling and he touched it with his fingertips. He poked his tongue between his teeth and touched that as well. Everything seemed to be working again, but he dared not try to speak just yet – in case he couldn't. However, he was brave enough to swing his legs clear of the bed and to stand up in the ridiculous green shirt. Finding his balance unimpaired he pulled on his trousers and laughed at the ease with which he managed it. Aware that he'd made an involuntary sound, he thought it worth trying to speak a word on purpose. 'Ha!' he said. 'Ha! Haaa!' then, 'Richard!'

That accomplished, he crossed the room to a cupboard whose doors had developed a slight outward bulge from

7

the weight of cargo it contained. Many things he wasn't looking for tumbled out on the floor: a pile of blankets, two garishly covered cushions, an acupuncture chart, two empty cans joined by a length of wire and several other pieces of domestic bric-a-brac. Wedged at the back of the lower portion of the cupboard he found his guitar and joyfully pulled it out. The strings were all attached but slack. Martin dragged some of the blankets to the middle of the floor and settled himself on them to tune the guitar. He'd progressed to making it play a passable chord when he heard his mother coming upstairs.

Fear gripped him, but he forced himself to keep looking at the door. He'd know at the first instant she appeared. She would be the first person he had seen since his collapse the previous morning. The heavy, plodding footsteps came nearer and Martin wanted to close his eyes against an awful possibility. Then the door swung open and he saw her. And the flame was there. The young man let his body sag with the overwhelming relief. His mother barged in carrying the loaded breakfast tray.

Startled, she exclaimed, 'Oh, my God! You're up!' Martin continued strumming and Beatrice carefully laid the tray on the seat of the bedside chair before approaching him directly. 'Martin! Can you hear me?' Martin smiled, nodded and laid down the guitar. His mother sighed. 'Ah, well there's that, anyway.' Noting his smile she felt entitled to be sterner. 'You shouldn't be up. You were to rest. Here, come and take your breakfast.' She assessed the eating arrangements. 'We'll have to get a table in here – a small table – if you're stayin'. There's room enough now with Richard in his own...' The guitarist suddenly sprang to his feet and strode to the door. Beatrice cried, 'Martin!' He raised his eyebrows and pointed across the landing to the bathroom. 'Oh! Oh, yes. Well, hurry up then; this'll get cold.'

As soon as Martin was out of the room the expression on his mother's face changed; possibly to one he'd never seen. The firm assertive lines drooped, her eyes clouded with worry and the upright combative stance which everyone thought natural to her was seen as a stiffly maintained façade. Her body sagged and, as she looked

8

around the room, her hands fidgeted with the tie of her apron. She went back to look at the breakfast things. Sitting on the edge of the bed she decided to pour him a cup of tea. It was when she picked up the sugar bowl that the once familiar pattern hit a block. She sat, bowl in hand, until Martin came back and then angrily shouted at him, 'How am *I* to know if you take sugar now or not? In your tea!'

'I take sugar.'

She rose quickly and moved to him. 'You can talk!'

'I take sugar and I can talk,' said Martin, sitting by the tray.

'Oh, that's a relief.'

'Whether or not I will, though, is another matter.'

'What hap...'

'Not yet!' said Martin picking up the knife and fork. 'You talk.'

The invitation provided a welcome dam-burst as far as Beatrice was concerned. But she began, 'What can I say until I know what happened, and you won't tell me. Oh, my heart's roasted over this. I've been exhausted with worry.' Martin smiled and, with a gesture of his fork, indicated that she should pull up a chair. She did so, banging it into position with a great show of annoyance.

'I don't suppose you're used to havin' breakfast. Now. Not a pick on you. What was I to think? Collapsed in a trance and speechless you were, not knowin' who had you by the arm or where your feet were placed. Not knowin'. And grippin' that bag so hard I had to prise your fingers loose. Locked! Why? Even when you were senseless you wouldn't let go of it. And goin' where? On the steps of the station, says Felix. From top to bottom. Might have split your skull open. And not another soul moved an inch, says he. Maybe they thought you were drunk too. But injured! Surely that matters? Not a soul. I don't know what the world's comin' to. Lucky he recognised you and didn't know you'd shifted from here.' Her attention was briefly diverted by the way Martin was dealing with the bacon. 'I cut the fat *off* that before I brought it up – so don't start *knittin'* at it!' She waited until he'd swallowed an unconsidered mouthful before resuming her former tone.

9

'It was a shock, I'll tell you. It was a shock that when I see you at *all* in three years you didn't know who faced you. Like a time-stretched infant; and had to put you to bed again.' Martin plucked questioningly at the shoulder of his sleeping garment. 'That's your Da's. Your own clothes were drenched in sweat. God knows what he would have said if he'd been here to see you the other morn.'

'Why have you kept my father's clothes?'

'Because there was *use* in them still. And the thought one of you at least might have fitted them when the time came. Some hope! Richard they might fit, if he was not so consaity, but you – never.'

'Though I'm not conceited.'

'How could you be conceited with a body like that?' she felt free to enquire, since he was part of her body – though he had not kept it well. 'Will ya tell me what has happened to you?'

'I heard Richard's voice.'

'He was here. I told him. Naturally he came to see how you were.'

'From his work?'

'Before his work.'

Martin smiled. 'Ah! So he'll have no broken time.' This was an old and mutually relished area of friction between the brothers, and Martin wished Richard might have been there to hear the dig at his tireless advocacy of hard work and good time-keeping.

But his mother – who always took Richard's side in such arguments – did not appreciate the witticism. 'He was worried. He *is* worried as *I* am. Is it too much to ask how you got into that state?'

'I was going away. For good.'

'Not come back! At all?'

Martin shook his head.

'Where?'

'If it's for always, "where" doesn't matter.'

'Without a word?' Beatrice tried to convey the enormity of this by a rapt tone of voice.

But her son was not to be coerced and continued briskly, 'Without two words: good-bye. And avoiding that strait-jacket I get stuck with a ... tent!'

Beattie was combative again. 'Think yourself lucky! You could have been clapped in a hospital – and maybe will be.'

'Not with you guarding the door Beatrice, darlin'. A light at the foot of the stairs and the lullaby, "Shut up!"'

His mother had not nearly finished exposing the gravity of his plan.

To her, never to come back was like dying. 'You could go away, and have it decided you'd not come back, and say nothin' of it?'

'I thought I could.' He laid his knife and fork on the plate and walked across the room.

Against her better judgment, Beatrice succumbed to a feeling of tenderness for the long-necked, narrow-shouldered, skinny young man intently staring out of the window. She moved to sit on the bed so that she could see him better. There was no denying he had not turned out the way she'd hoped. In fact, he'd thrown away the opportunities which she, then Richard, had made sacrifices to give him. All that he had to show for his fine education was that he spoke nicely. That would have been one in the eye for the neighbours if there had been any neighbours left who mattered a damn. But almost as soon as he came back from university he'd gone off on his own. No. Not even on his own. He'd chosen to live with that girl. Then suddenly he was making trinkets like a common tinker and she never saw him at all. It seemed to his mother a bewildering waste – the boy just drifting with no clear end in view. And now this breakdown or whatever it was. Both her sons, it seemed, were less strong than she. And she was by no means as strong as she had been. The resolution which had kept her going when the children were young was not, she found, a renewable asset. She called softly, 'Martin!'

He turned to face her, overbright and somehow forbidding. 'Yes?'

She glared at him and loudly declared, 'Will you hell!' She plunged a hand into her pocket and took out her cigarettes. While she lit up, Martin paced slowly to and fro – as though the transfer of his weight from one foot to the other was in itself an accomplishment worth enjoying.

11

Beatrice puffed away in silence for several minutes, hoping that Martin would feel obliged to compromise his plans for desertion. But he just went on pacing from one side of the room to the other, so she spoke up again. 'You're not right or you'd never think of such a thing. And anyway, the doctor will be in to see you again.'

'*Again!*' He sank once more upon the blankets as though overcome with incredulity. '*You* called a doctor! The first doctor to set foot in this house, and I missed him.' Snatching up his guitar he started to sing to the tune of 'Johnny Lad'.

'Oh doctors are a race of men
I do not recognise
They cut out vital parts for fun
And tell you not to rise
But wi' you, And wi' you
I'm wi' you Johnnie Lad
I'll dance the bachles off me feet
Wi' you ma Johnnie Lad.
I've danced the bachles off me feet
For you ... ma ... John ... nie Lad.' He strummed wildly to underline the message. 'Escape Beatrice, Ma. That's the thing.'

His Ma regarded him without amusement and adopted as implacable a posture as the unstable edge of the bed would permit. 'If you don't want to tell me, I'll ask you no more.'

'I don't want to tell you because the difference between what I tell and what you hear is too great.'

'That'll be because I'm so ignorant, I suppose. Though I scrubbed hard for the education *you* have.'

'Oh God! Not the Old Mother Riley bit?'

Beatrice threw him a withering look then pushed herself off the bed taking a last long drag of her cigarette. She threw it out of the window.

Martin protested, 'No wonder the wash-house drain gets clogged. Your fag-ends must be thick on the roof there.'

'Nothin' of the kind. I'm rarely in this room now ... since I've been left.'

'Christ!'

12

'Mind your tongue.'

'Oh, I forgot. I forgot which of the thousand names of God you'll entertain at home.'

Beatrice stuck to the point. 'Between what you tell and I hear – what is the difference?'

'Time.' He nodded vehemently to impress the point. 'Whatever I say – you'll hear me saying it at sixteen or eighteen. But I'm really saying it ten years later and you haven't got there yet. So – the sense of what I am, *now*, cannot get through.'

'I can understand that.'

'Can you?'

'Oh, surely, I can understand it. But I don't *believe* it. You look just the same to me.'

'On the outside.' He smiled ruefully as he looked down at himself. 'For that's another difficulty. The inside no longer matches the outside. Disowns it! They could well part company altogether.'

'Avoid it then, by gettin' more chuck down ya,' Beatrice advised. 'You've not been eatin' enough to keep body and soul together. Little wonder it is you're light-headed.'

Martin grinned and replied imitating her brogue, 'Oh, it's right you are Beattie, girl! There's nothin' for keepin' a fella earthbound so fast as food.' He ducked out of range as she swiped at his head then added more soberly in his own voice, 'And family. And home.'

'And what else matters?'

'If only that were all.'

'Well? Are ya goin' to tell me what's the matter with you?'

'The matter is,' said Martin slowly, 'that I can see more than is good for me to know. And I've seen a man who doesn't know he's dead.'

His mother's response was immediate and comforting, 'That's a lot of baloney.'

'I have seen that he is dead, probably for the rest of his life. And I feel as guilty as though I'd killed him.'

'You're an extravagant liar.'

But Martin was not put off by conventional terms, nor their apparent contradiction. He knew what he'd seen when he walked into that room. The familiar face was smiling, and welcoming, but the person was stark dead. A dark space where there should have been a flame. And he realised beyond any doubt that the person he was depending on for advice on how to use his sudden ability had no use for it himself; and no means to recognise it. With little regard for his mother's comprehension Martin added, 'I just could not pretend he was still alive when I could *see* he was dead.'

'You're ravin'.'

'No. Though that would make it easier.' Beatrice turned impatiently towards the door and Martin made an effort to convey some idea of what was at stake. 'Listen! I've often heard you say, when an ailing person refuses to quit – "He has more life in him than body to carry it."'

'Oh, that's true enough.'

'Yes. And it's true as well that the spirit in someone can sicken or die while the body is still healthy and young.'

Beatrice regarded him evenly. 'It's possible, I suppose.'

'Well,' Martin told her, 'that's what I can see, now – what I can't *help* seeing.'

His mother appeared to be thinking of what he'd told her, but really she was not. She said, 'You'd better have a bath before the doctor comes. I'll stoke up the kitchen fire for the hot water.' She paused with her hand on the door-knob. 'You'll have a hard job gettin' shot of us!' she declared.

'So it seems,' Martin sighed. He listened to her feet descending all fifteen of the steps. He counted them. Then, left in silence, the overpowering image of what called him flooded into his mind again and he lost all consciousness of familiar surroundings. It was stronger now than it had been before. Every time it returned there was more clarity in it and more urgency. The waves brimmed higher and higher on the shore. The suction pulling the water back became less and less. He had very little time.

Perhaps I ought to make it clear that I am not imagining what took place in that house. That is, I'm not inventing it. I made it my business to find out exactly what happened and listened very carefully to how those involved expressed themselves. Being Dubliners, they had no difficulty in doing that. I know, therefore, it was about an hour after Martin finished his breakfast that Kate Shevelin's car moved uncertainly along the terrace as she tried to make out the house numbers – many of which had long since been erased. Kate knocked at the front door and waited. She was a bright, pretty girl in her early twenties. Well able to take care of herself, she still felt some trepidation at going where she knew she wasn't wanted. And Beatrice confirmed that she wasn't wanted by just giving a grunt of recognition and waving her upstairs with an impatient gesture. Martin was sitting cross-legged on a pile of blankets, apparently asleep. The girl advanced into the room and said, 'Martin! Are you all right?'

'Hello, Kate.'

'Are you well?'

'I'm not well *used*. Yet.' He patted the blanket and smiled up at her. 'Join me.'

As she got down she indicated the prominently placed hold-all. 'That's new.'

'And broken,' Martin noticed, 'by the look of it.'

'We have...' That was wrong. 'We' was what was in question. She started again in a lighter manner. 'There is a suitcase of mine you could have used.'

His smile faded abruptly. 'Kate. Do not. Do not. *Don't* be calm and long suffering.' He rolled away from her and got to his feet. 'Who sent for you?'

'Nobody sent for me. Richard stopped to tell me you were here and not well.' Kate laughed, eager still to impose lightness on the situation. 'What he said was that you'd have one of your "turns".'

'Oh, I have. A new and radical turn I certainly have had.'

'I think he meant one of your "blackouts".'

'No doubt.'

Kate began to feel angry at the brisk, bantering tone he was adopting. It was one thing for her to try and keep it light but if he insisted on the same strategy her point would be lost. 'You don't want to see me.' He gave no indication either way. 'I only came because I thought you were ill.'

15

'That's very discriminating.'

Finding herself left high and dry on the blankets in the middle of the room, Kate was uneasy. In carefully relaxed movements she got to her feet. 'But I was wrong. Obviously, you're enjoying yourself. Again. The freedom, I suppose.' She moved casually to the breakfast tray and started nibbling decorously at what Martin had left. 'Would you have written? If you hadn't been overcome on the way, I mean. Would you have told me you weren't coming back? Because that's it, isn't it Martin? It's not that difficult. You wasted money on the bag. And if you actually bought a ticket for somewhere … *unn*ecessary.' She plumped herself down on the edge of the bed with an air of smug defiance. Seeing her settle, Martin crossed to the door and firmly closed it while bracing himself for what had to be done. Kate took his action as a good sign. 'Oh! I would have done that only your mother was hovering and she …' An incongruous possiblity struck her. 'You didn't *intend* to come back to her did you?'

'No. She got me back by accident. A friend of the family who didn't know I had a loose woman elsewhere.'

'Only one?'

'Stop fishing.'

'Anyway, I'm sure your mother was glad to get rid of you.'

'And you?'

'No.' Kate leaned back across the bed, resting on her elbows. 'No, I'm not glad. But I accept it. That was the bargain. No hassle. No certificate of ownership. If one or the other had enough, or got bored – he or she would blow. And you weren't obliged to give notice, either.'

'Or give reasons.'

'Or give reasons,' Kate conceded.

'But …?'

'Yes. But! I'm glad you brought that up. *But* it would help, or be comforting, or less damaging, at least – to know that there were reasons.'

'There is a reason.'

'Another girl?'

Martin chuckled and drew closer to sit beside her on the

bed. 'Kate. Kate! How can you be so clever and use it only as a front?'

'That's not a fault. That's cunning. Well? Are you going to live with another girl?'

'I'm not going to live with anybody. Or I wasn't going to.'

'You've changed your mind.'

'I was forestalled. Why, *I* wonder. Or have wondered, you'll understand, at waking under the eye of Beatrice and again under your eye. To wake twice in the same morning to the same question differently put, sets me wondering. She wants to know "Where?" You want to know "Who?" And I've still to get an answer to my preference of "Why?". Why was I forestalled? Blocked? What is it that I've to do which I haven't done?'

'You're not making sense.'

'That may be part of it. But it *was* done. A few steps more and I would have been on the bus. Away. Accomplished.'

'I don't know what you're talking about.'

He threw back his head to sing softly, '"I don't know where I'm goin', I don't know who'd go with me, I know who I love, but God knows I won't marry."' He thumped the complaining springs of the bed and moved swiftly to a small bookcase fronted by glass sliding panels. They did not slide readily, having accumulated so much dust in their tracks. 'Isn't it remarkable! Beatrice has not read a book in her life, yet she has kept all these of mine.' He knelt in front of the shelves and started removing books. 'In the covers I made for them. Grocery wrappings.' He turned to look over his shoulder at Kate who was regarding him with an amused but neutral expression from the bed. 'Do you know, I used to iron the brown paper to make covers for books that were never new. There are books here I never read, but kept because I was sure they'd be invaluable. And the ones I wanted to read again, I could never find because I'd lent them to somebody else.'

'Not to me.'

'No. You could buy them for yourself. Maybe that's my unfulfilled mission. A pyre! Rid Beatrice of maintaining my *Rubaiyat*, my Blake, my essence of Donne, my Emerson ...' As he pulled the books out on the rug the last one fell open at a page where it had been held open many times in the past. Crouched over it on his hands and knees, Martin read a stanza:

'"They reckon ill who leave me out;
When me they fly, I am the wings;
I am the doubter and the doubt,
And I the hymn the Brahmin sings."'

He snapped it shut. 'I should get rid of them all – today! And I will, if I can find out why she has kept them. What use are they now?'

Kate went to join him at the bookcase. She stood behind him and stroked his jaw and behind his ears. 'Maybe one of Richard's boys would like them.'

'That's it!'

'When he gets older.'

'They're for one of Richard's boys – when he gets older, and feels inclined; which he'd *better* if she's kept them for him.'

She leaned forward, allowing her breast to press against his shoulders, and kissed his temple. 'Maybe not.'

'Or maybe not.'

'It could be...' She knelt beside him and kissed his mouth. 'Beatrice thought you'd come back.' Martin responded to the kiss and with his free hand caressed the back of her neck under her hair.

'Oh, yes! No member of the family is ever lost until dead. Her age scale is out of...' The word was going to be 'focus' but it got lost in another long kiss. The imprint of the kiss itself brought into play the whole delightful ritual which had been the prelude to their love-making in the past. Their bodies, unaware that this was a quite different occasion, responded with automatic ease. Martin succumbed to the pleasure of it and, for a few moments, that was enough.

Kate pushed him away a little but felt secure enough to say, 'She knew I'd be no good for you.'

'She was wrong there, too.'

'Really?'

'Oh, Kate!'

'Sorry. Yes. She was wrong.'

'While I was *with* you.' Martin gently relinquished his hold of her and got to his feet. 'Well,' he rubbed his hands with brisk satisfaction, 'that was very pleasant. That's – the suitcase, and no competition, the books, and Richard's boys and...'

'And me!' Kate glared up at him.

'Oh! Are you going to be angry? Please feel free.'

'Angry? No. But I can *not* understand why you should seem so pleased about this happening.'

'Happening?'

'Leaving.'

'You'd like a decent show of regret.'

Again finding herself isolated on the floor, Kate rose to face him; this time with less grace but a good deal more energy. 'I'd like a decent explanation.'

'"You'll never have to explain," she said.'

'Not that I want any plain or cockeyed reasons for what you're doing, or why you're doing it, or where you should be. That's yours. And this boyish gaiety you seem to have picked up...'

'"No reasons. No notice."' Martin continued quoting to her in a level, bland voice while her tone grew steadily more heated, and louder.

'... *regressed* into – you can keep that too. Yours. Wherever you got it – all yours. I go no further than yesterday. But yesterday and three years before yesterday is mine. May I be allowed to tie that up to my satisfaction?'

'"No ties or claims or certificates of ownership,"' he quoted.

'I know you like things to be tidy. Maybe take in the day before yesterday. Can you stretch to that? Okay? Was that an act? Had everything changed then and you were pretending? You are damn all good at pretending. It couldn't be.'

'That's true. So if...'

Her interruption rode angrily over whatever sophistry he might employ. 'And *worry!* Among all the nice negative virtues we agreed on, surely "No worry" was one. Hm? Wasn't that in there?' Kate started pacing in an arc which from all points in her progress reflected directly on Martin.

'Well? How did I feel then, in that empty flat last night? Not knowing where you were. Not that I had to know where you were ... but not knowing if you were ... safe. Or hurt.'

'Or alive.'

'Yes! Oh, for God's sake Martin, don't close up. You could have been killed.'

'They would have told you'.

'*Who* would have told me? When you fainted or collapsed or whatever it was, they brought you here.'

'And Richard told you.'

'In *passing*. On his way to work.'

'If I'd been killed he might have taken the whole morning off. We've never had enough time together.'

'We've had three very happy years.'

'I meant, Richard and me.' Kate stood rock still and he quickly went on, 'But you're right. We have been happy, too.'

'So –' She resumed pacing the arc but on a wider radius. 'How could it all end in one day? You'll not deny that for you to leave me there's got to be a very big attraction.'

'And there is. The trouble seems to be, keeping it in view. Keeping an eye on it, gleaming ahead.' He moved so suddenly towards her that she collided with him. And his steadying gesture became an embrace. 'My dear and darling Kate, without you I wouldn't be in a position to see it at all. I'm sorry for the worry. I am. I am sorry. And the suddenness.'

She threw her arms around his neck but as he hugged her he realised, with a certainty which was both clear and sad, that it was only for her sake he was sorry. He found himself incapable of being sorry on his own account, even though the warmth and happiness they'd shared had been fully shared. But it lay behind him now, like a fondly remembered cocoon. He could no more fold himself into it again than a butterfly could re-enter its own chrysalis. As the warmth of Kate's body pressed against him he regretted that her happiness seemed to depend so much upon him and, almost involuntarily, he exclaimed, 'Oh! I wish you were happy to *you*. Shining in!' She stepped back from him but he, unaware that he was talking nonsense, was compelled by an inner burst of certainty to go on. 'Not reflecting, but shining as yourself. You have done it. I know it is possible. But can you do it now?' He stretched his arms as though touching might help her to understand him. 'There is a word. Yes, I used to know the word when I didn't really know the meaning. And now when the meaning blazes at me, the word has gone.' He swayed wildly from side to side and shook his head. 'I should sit down and let it come to me. But that – what that word says – is what we all deserve to be. Shining for our own sake.' Another gust of energy seemed to shake him and more words tumbled out. 'How *can* I sit down when every part of me works, and is well, and is waiting … waiting … to begin. To *begin*!'

Kate said, 'If you'd taken the suitcase I would have known you were leaving.'

'I didn't want to take anything of yours.'

'What?'

'Things, I mean.'

Kate stared at him in disbelief, then exploded. 'Oh, my good Christ! *Things*! He worries about things. My things!' She went storming around the room, pulling open drawers and plucking objects out of the cupboard and rifling the bookcase. 'What about these marvellous un-breakable things you left *her* to moulder and rot? Books she won't read, a guitar she can't play. Blankets enough for the coldest night there's ever been.' She kicked at them. 'This room is stuffed and hung with things you parted with for me. What makes you think I'd be tight-fisted about *things*? What is so valuable about my bloody suitcase that you shouldn't take it?'

'Kate!'

'As a hint. Apart from saving me the worry and a sleepless night – a clue! Or is that too much for you to … for you to …' Kate tried desperately to fight off the bout of weeping which was mounting steadily in her chest. 'Honest to God, Martin – do you think you left me with everything I …? That you took nothing? Nothing!' She surrendered to the tears and threw herself face-down across the bed, sobbing.

Martin went at once to comfort her. He stroked and

21

massaged her shoulders for a few moments in silence and then he murmured, 'It isn't easy to do *anything* well. I thought I might meet you at lunch-time. But before that… It became impossible.'

Kate's nose was pressed against the pillow but probably her muffled question was, 'Why?'

'I had to get away without seeing you. Without seeing anyone else. I was wrong but I couldn't take the chance. Just fear. I had to get away.' And, rather bravely in the circumstances, he added, 'I still have to. *Today*.'

But Kate's attention had been taken by an earlier statement. She lifted her head and turned a little to face him. 'Fear? Of me?'

'Of what you might have become. I didn't want it to happen with you. I didn't want it to happen at all!'

Kate twisted round more completely and allowed Martin to support her. 'What can change in one day?' she asked.

'Kate, we always knew there would be such a day.' This was not at all the same thing he'd been talking about before. Martin knew it, but knew also that Kate was not in the best frame of mind to take the truth. 'There could only be one day when this might happen. Leading up to it gradually must be worse. Mm?'

'Maybe. But I'd have liked the chance to lead you *away* from it – gradually.' She sniffed and started looking for her handkerchief. It was a measure of the trust they'd had in each other that she did not disguise the unattractive sniffs or her ruined make-up. 'I could have.'

'No. You couldn't. Believe me. Though if I could have done it better I would have. And should have, I suppose. Maybe that's why I was brought back to you and those here.' He looked carefully at her wide and reddened eyes. 'Kate? Is there any way I could go, and you'd be happy?'

To the girl, that was patently a stupid question. 'No!'

'Now, you mean. But is there any way it would be all right afterwards?'

She shook her head. 'How can that be? You were brought back, you said. Doesn't that mean you should stay? That you were wrong? Doesn't it?'

'I wish I knew.'

'Stay and you'll know.'

'I mean, I wish I knew how to do it well.'

Kate freed herself from his embrace and some of her former annoyance returned. 'What brought this *on*?'

'Wrong question again. "Who?"' He lay back on the bed. '"Who?" is the question you want.'

'But you said there wasn't anyone!'

'I said there wasn't another girl, and I wasn't making for somebody else's bed.'

'But somebody else *is* involved?'

'That – and a feeling which grows stronger all the time. An urgent, unanswerable feeling.' He groaned at the inadequacy of the description. 'Del Morrisey was just the trigger for that.'

'Del Morrisey? Isn't he the man who owns the shed where you work?'

'The very same. And he is "who".'

The door opened and Beatrice returned to collect the breakfast tray. Crossing the room she frostily noted the junk which Kate had strewn around. She said, 'The water will be warm enough now for a bath. If you use plenty of cold.'

'What do you think of Kate, Ma? Give your blind prejudice a shake and tell me what she looks like to you.'

'Look at the mess. Have yis been tryin' to wreck the place?'

Martin pointed a damning finger at Kate. 'She did it.' As Beatrice laid the tray down again and picked up a book which had slithered under the chair, Martin insisted on an opinion. 'Eh? What do you think, now you see her?'

Kate mumbled apologetically, 'We were having an argument.'

Beatrice grunted, 'Uh, huh.' Then, as Kate started to tidy up, she grew more assertive. 'You can leave it to me. I know where everything goes'. She gave Martin a pointed stare. 'The water, I said. If you're havin' a bath, the water's ready.'

'I heard you, Beatrice, and I'm giving it a lot of thought. But I'd like you to know each other. It would pain me to think there'd be any awkward silence or unease when I'm gone. Introductions! What am I thinking of? Introductions, of course! Otherwise you never know who you might meet.'

Kate felt unequal to the double assault. 'I was just leaving. And we met at the front door.'

'The front door, child, doesn't count,' Martin chided. 'This is a social occasion. Eh, Beatrice? You know that. Beattie knows that. This is a single-bed bedroom social occasion and something of a rescue operation. What could you say at the front door that would set anybody's mind at ease?'

His mother interrupted warningly, 'Martin, this is not kind.'

'It is not. It is not, I confess. But decorum has the upper hand at the moment; with me standin' barefoot in me Da's shirt because you've hidden me underthings.'

'I washed your underwear and it's drying.'

'Spoken with rare diplomacy. A perfect opening gambit. Oh, you're getting the hang of it already. Now, Kate, I would like you to meet my mother who thinks I should have more than one set of underwear and holds you responsible.'

'Me! But you always...'

'Mother, may I introduce Kate – a quite undomesticated girl of good education – with whom I have been living; and dying, by inches.'

'I had the impression you enjoyed it,' the girl said.

'Enjoying it doesn't alter the fact.' To his mother he added soberly, 'But that we have enjoyed it is something you should know – and now can see why.'

'I have seen ... Kate, before now,' his mother allowed.

'Had her pointed out, you mean.'

'Did you?' Kate asked incredulously.

'Of course she did. Thought of reporting you to the NSPCC – because there's not a pick *on* me.' He gave a bellow of laughter and swaggered to the door. 'Well that's my little chore done. Too bad spiderman Richard is otherwise engaged, but what with this gathering, the prospect of bath and a renegade doctor imminent, my mornings are getting crowded enough.' He went out and closed the door behind him.

Beatrice shook her head wearily. 'He's feverish, I think.'

'Maybe. A "rescue operation". To rescue him, I suppose. That's what he said.'

'I've never much listened to what he said. He talks a lot of nonsense, y'know, at times.'

'But a rescue would make sense.'

'If he was drowning, maybe.'

'Will he be all right in there?'

'Havin' a bath!'

'It might affect his... temperature... Affect his balance. And if the door's locked...'

'There's no lock on the door.' Having cleared away everything that would create an actual obstruction, Beatrice decided the room was tidy enough. She folded her arms and nodded to Kate. 'You're a teacher.'

'Yes. Very young children.'

'He was lucky there.'

'Pardon?'

'A good steady wage, I mean. He can't make much with what he plays at.'

'Oh, he makes quite a lot.'

'I'm talkin' about money, not brooches.'

'I thought ... no. No, he doesn't sell much. But he could sell more. He makes very beautiful jewellery,' Kate said.

'Maybe if he didn't satisfy himself so much he'd sell more. He's finicky. Always was. What he does, he does to please himself instead of tryin' to please whoever might buy it.'

'Yes, that's true.'

'There's no need to tell me what's true about Martin.'

'You're right.' The girl hastily corrected any impression that she'd a mind of her own. 'Is that better?'

'Hm.' Beatrice moved the tray onto the bed and sat in the vacated chair. There established, she dug out her cigarettes and lit up.

'Mrs Doyle,' Kate began. Beatrice gave her a quick glance through shrewd eyes crinkled against tobacco smoke. But she said nothing and Kate tried again, 'Mrs Doyle, I was going to...'

'Yes. I heard ya. And I think we could ... and better together than separately.'

'What?' the girl asked.

'What you were going to say.'

'But I didn't.' Kate was startled. 'I haven't suggested anything yet.'

'Then I've saved you the bother.'

'But how do you know?'

The woman brushed the lap of her apron. 'It's not necessary to *say* everything to know it, surely?'

'That's true. I mean, you are right. Certainly.'

'It's a matter of *where* we can get him to stay.'

'We have to convince him first.'

'A waste of time tryin'. Much better just stop him goin'.'

Kate could not suppress a gurgle of laughter. 'How long could you keep that up?'

'Until he feels the urge to get back to you. Until he has a natural purpose that's stronger than this whim.'

'Mrs Doyle, I really never thought of myself as a "natural purpose" in your scheme of things.'

'Not mine. His. But what else could you think to be? There bein' no children, or marriage.'

'Whatever it was, I'm beginning to lose sight of it already. Has he had "whims" like this before?'

'Of one kind or another.' Beatrice sighed at the recollection of so many instances, but selected one. 'Until he was twelve or so he thought for certain he was a changeling.'

'A *what*?'

'Change-ling. Honest to God. Convinced of it, he was; and kept lookin' at his ears in the mirror. Can you believe that?' She gravely exhaled a jet of smoke. 'He wasn't, of course.' Kate gave a burst of laughter and the woman glared at her, adding, 'But a difficult child to rear.'

'I wish I could have seen him when he was young.'

'You can see signs of him. Look there!' She pointed her cigarette to the wall by the window. 'His footprints showin' through.'

'He walked up the *wall*?' Kate gulped and switched her attention sharply from the wall to see if the woman could possibly be serious.

'Over the paper. Time and again. Two years old he was, or three, when his Da and I were paperin' his room. We laid the paper on the floor to paste the back and he kept walkin' over it, watching where his feet had been. Highly delighted.' She nodded towards the wall. 'We didn't notice that strip until it was too late.'

Kate moved close to the ancient wallpaper and did clearly make out the shapes. 'Such tiny feet.'

'Oh, he had just learned to walk at the time.' Beatrice's voice took on a softer tone. 'You're fond of childer?'

'Oh, yes!'

'You should have one or two of your own.'

'I would.'

'I see.'

'Probably.'

There was no denying the sadness in the girl's voice and Beatrice cast around for something to change the subject. 'A towel! He's nothing to dry himself.' She got up and rummaged through a couple of drawers. There were no towels but she thought a brown, chenille table-cover would do.

'I'll give it to him.' Kate extended her hand.

For a moment the impropriety stalled Beatrice. 'Oh! All right. And tell him to use the mat when he gets out.'

Kate slung the table-cover over her shoulder and crossed the landing to the bathroom. The door was wide open. The bath was wet but the plug still dangled from the tap. She ran back to report to Beatrice, 'He's not there!'

'In the bathroom?'

'He's gone.'

'Where could he go with only trousers, a shirt and nothing to his feet.' She hurried from the room and went downstairs calling, 'Martin! Martin! Are you there? Martin!' While the brief search went on downstairs Kate went to the window and craned her neck to look all around. Beatrice returned and announced, 'He's not in the house.'

'And no sign of him in the street.'

'After me heatin' the water, he ran it down the drain. What'll the doctor say? The boy can't be well.'

'But he's certainly determined.'

Beatrice grasped at a straw. 'Unless there's somebody else he had to see – and just remembered.'

'And couldn't remember his *shoes*!'

27

'Maybe you could catch up with him.'

'I wouldn't try. He seems to have made up his mind.'

The woman dismissed that with a sharp flick of her hand. 'He's feverish. His mind's not to be trusted.'

Kate was not prepared to be so cavalier. 'Whether you trust it or not, he does.'

'Do you? Do you believe all the nonsense he's been ramblin' since he woke? You're more used to him now than me. Is this how he is?'

'Only on what he calls his "good days",' said Kate, smiling at the recollection.

'*Good*? What's good about drivin' those that have care of him half out o' their wits?'

'Mm. His good days were usually my bad days.' The girl sighed. 'Even so, his being happy is what I remember about them.'

Thwarted, Beatrice resumed her place on the chair and shifted the blame. 'I think you've been too soft with him. It doesn't do in the long run.'

'The long run doesn't come up. We are day to day.'

'Well, ya know I haven't approved of you and Martin.'

'I know that, yes.'

'Things are too much the man's way if all the woman can count on is formin' a habit.'

Kate gave a slight gasp of incredulity then stated, 'Mrs Doyle, I may accept the position as a "natural purpose" but I'm damned if I'll be called "a hopeful habit".'

'Isn't that the only link wit' him you could claim?'

'I love him.'

'I expect *so*. And that is somethin' you are free to do. It's what *he* is free to do must be prepared for.'

'He is free to do as he pleases. We agreed.'

'Then why are you so ill-prepared?'

'I'm upset because I ... care for him. For what happens to him.'

Beatrice showed a tight triumphant smile. 'So – your fine free agreement would only work if you *didn't* care for him. And by that time you should have children to care for; free or not.'

'He refuses.'

'Ah! Then it seems clear to me that if you want children

28

you should have found a man who wants them, too.'

Though feeling the subject out of place, Kate asked, 'What about love?'

'The children will last longer,' said Beatrice, with no fear of contradiction.

'Is that the agreement you made, Mrs Doyle?'

'That's none o' yer business.'

'No. I don't suppose it is. But you give hard advice to take without proof.'

'Proof! Like a marriage certificate, you mean? That kind of proof? I have *that*.'

'Martin's right. You're a wintry woman.'

'It comes gradually,' said Beatrice. 'Didn't he tell you anything at all about the cause of this?'

'He said it was something to do with Del Morrisey.'

'Morrisey, is it? Oh, he's a twister, that bucky.'

'Is he? I thought Martin was very friendly with him,' Kate said.

'More fool, he. Old Morrisey knew Martin's father, as I've cause to remember. Still, I can't see them fittin' the case.'

'No, I suppose not.' The girl sighed. 'But that was the only name he mentioned.'

Beatrice produced the visiting card from the pocket of her apron. 'More likely to be mixed up with *this*!' She handed it to Kate. 'It … dropped out of his pocket when I was undressin' him.'

Kate examined the crisp, elegantly engraved card which bore only a name, an address and a telephone number. 'Do you know who it is?'

'I do not; but I'd dearly like to know.'

'Why don't you phone him?'

Beatrice gave her an offended stare. 'I have no *phone*. And there's not one complete instrument for miles around here.'

Kate decided. 'I'll do it then; from the flat.'

'*Would* you? To London?'

'Yes. Of course.'

'And you'll tell me what the man says?'

Kate nodded. 'I'll come back.'

29

It was nearly half past eleven when Martin reached the building site. Many people had seen him as he ran towards it – a barefoot young man pounding along the pavements with the loose sleeves of his green shirt flapping around his thin arms. Many more people saw him when he reached his goal. A crowd gathered outside the protective fence of the site to watch the odd figure climbing; first on the staging ladders and then on the bare girders of the towering steel frame. His long blond hair was whipped by the wind as he rose higher. There was an increasing chorus of shouts from the ground. They tried to attract the attention of the erectors standing on top of the structure who were all dressed in tough fabric overalls, cinched at ankles and wrists, secured by heavy leather belts and wearing blue helmets. The erectors looked down at the gathering circle of tiny upturned faces. Faintly, they heard the shouts. Then, looking closer, they noticed the small climbing figure who approached them with frightening disregard for his own safety. The crowd saw one of the tiny helmeted figures detach himself from the others and slowly edge down in the direction of the climber. The rescuer looked like a spider crawling from the apex of a web. And suddenly he dropped like a spider in a sheer, swift descent, arrested only by the thread which held him.

It was Richard who, encumbered by a spare safety harness, abseiled down the broad central riser. The two figures on the maze of girders drew closer together – the descending one moving in sudden precise leaps, the other inching slowly up; crawling on a diagonal strut. They met at a point more than halfway up the structure. The crowd strained to see what was happening as the two figures merged. Then they gasped as a gesticulating blob detached itself from the main support and the thread which had seemed too slender to support one man was seen to be supporting both. They were gradually lowered to safety.

Richard laid his brother on the ground and unhitched the harness. The younger man was breathless, torn and bloody but apparently in good spirits. Richard stared at him in a tense fury. The first thing was to get him out of there, but the car was about quarter of a mile away in a car park outside the site, to be clear of dust and debris. He looked across the short distance to the perimeter fence and at the line of spectators who'd gathered. One of them was a short, middle-aged man getting out of a car. Richard picked up his brother in an awkward fireman's lift and staggered across the uneven ground to the fence. The driver of the car watched their progress with great interest and, when they were close enough, Richard asked him, 'Could you give us a lift?'

I said, 'Yes, of course,' and opened a rear door so that Martin could be bundled in to sprawl across the back seat. Richard got in beside me and gave me directions. 'And would ya hurry, before the Garda comes, or an ambulance.'

'I'll go as fast as I can. But would you point which is left and which is right for me?'

'God, man! Ya surely know your left from your right?'

'Only when I think about it,' I told him. 'And by then we could have passed a turning.'

'Okay. Will ya just reverse then, and get on to Manor Street, and go south?'

'Which way is south?'

'To your right. Or it will be to your right once you've turned back.' He sighed through gritted teeth. 'And your right is *that* way.' He held his hand in front of my eyes with a finger extended.

I nodded and executed a tyre-crunching three-point-turn. 'I think I was lost anyway.'

'I'm not a bit surprised.'

'What I was looking for was the Old Cabra Road. Do you know where that is?'

He nodded. 'I do. But it's little use to us at the moment; and in the wrong direction. What we want is to get down on the Quays.' He gave me a worried glance. 'They're along the riverside.'

'Yes. I should think they would be.'

When we reached a less complicated stretch of road, Martin piped up from the back seat, 'I saw you yesterday, didn't I?'

Richard shook his head. 'Did ya hell. Ye were dead to the world.'

'Not you! The man.'

31

I agreed. 'Yes. You collapsed just in front of me at the bus station.' The voice in the back of the back of the car chuckled. 'I never forget a flame.'

My reason for being in Dublin was to attend rehearsals of a play of mine which was part of the city's theatre festival held in March each year. It is principally a festival of drama, unlike the Edinburgh Festival which claims to be all things to all men but is really for the benefit of music and musicians. Dublin, then, is for the spoken word. And if you can hold your own in a city full of marvellous talkers there's little to fear if the play is transferred to London or New York – except, perhaps, that in those places they won't be able to *listen* quick enough.

The theatre we'd been assigned was the Eblana and it is housed in the basement of the bus terminal. On the previous morning, as I was crossing the concourse I'd noticed a young man with long, fair hair leaning against the low wall which shields the steep basement stairway. I assumed he was drunk. He gripped a canvas holdall and swayed on his feet, supporting himself against the wall. Just as I passed him to descend the stair he seemed to lose his grip and lurched against me. The impact had more effect on him than on me. He spun round, lost his footing, and tumbled all the way down the basement steps. But he fell limply so there was nothing broken and no sign of cuts, though he was stunned. Several people crowded into the narrow stairwell and one of them, evidently, was a friend of the young man who helped him to his feet. The friend supported him to a car and they drove off. I thought little about the incident and went on into the theatre which, like all theatres in the morning, was gloomy, dark and cold. The only illumination was from a single, harsh worklight above the stage. I spent the whole day there, sitting well back in the shadows and wincing.

The following morning was to be devoted to the 'first tech.' – a call I've learned never to answer. Apart from giving everyone a foretaste of purgatory, the avowed purpose of the technical rehearsal is to concentrate upon light cues, sound cues, music levels, property changes, costume changes, sticking doors, collapsible furniture and the timing of absolutely everything. Considering how essential it is to get these things right, the stage crew displays marvellous ingenuity in getting them wrong, again and again and again. It is a rehearsal when the actors count for nothing but are shunted on and off to change costumes with bewildering rapidity. Nor do they ever get to act a scene right through, but merely 'top and tail' while the gritty mechanics of putting the play on the stage claims the whole attention of the director – already hard pressed to prevent the lynching of the set designer. It is an exercise to discover just how much can get fouled up. Also, the subtle fabric of the piece constructed over many months is tested to destruction – several times. For whenever one thing is satisfactorily fixed three other things instantly go to pieces. It's like a mutiny in slow motion which goes on all day – and sometimes all night, if the budget will bear the overtime. I'd no intention of sitting through it merely to provide a minor target for the spleen of the stage manager, so I took the day off.

Thus I was able to watch the spectacular, abseiling rescue on the high girders. It was already well underway when I was stopped by the crowd obstructing the road. I'd decided to spend my free time on a jaunt to Ceanannus Mor to see the monastery where the Book of Kells was written. But that had to wait until another occasion – and better luck in finding the Old Cabra Road. My hired car was pressed into bloody service as a taxi. Martin's bare feet were severely cut and left dark imprints on the carpet over the transmission hump. It was not an easy thing to explain to Hertz, so I didn't try – though I did offer extra payment for cleaning. It seemed a small fee to place against the remarkable experience I'd gained from meeting the Doyle family.

Later, as I've mentioned, I used the experience to make a play based upon close questioning of all but one of the parties involved. Beatrice refused to talk to me. But the play did not really work very well for the general public in Dublin or in London, though one avid patron's reaction was to pursue me to New York several years later when I was busy with something else. Those for whom *The Only*

33

Street didn't work were disappointed because it was impossible to show the *purpose* of Martin's escape bid. And it was impossible to see how the story would end. All these years later, I know how it ends and how only the end reveals the purpose. Before I get to that, however, it might be helpful to outline what led to Martin's frightening insight and what he was doing which brought it about.

Martin claimed to be a jewel-maker – not a jeweller. That is, he was not in the retail trade of selling what others had designed and still others had manufactured. He was not a shop-keeper, though he did try to sell what he made. To my assertion that only the forces of nature can make a jewel, he replied that what nature makes are aberrant crystals; and does not make enough of them – or there would be no market for gems. Martin specialised in enamelling, because that was all he could afford. Silver or copper provided the base and mount but it was really out of coloured glass that the young man made jewels. They were intricate, immensely varied and very beautiful. Their high value lay not in the raw materials but in the fact that *he* had made them. I was forced to conclude that the difference between what jewellers offered and what Martin fashioned was the difference between tarting-up a commodity investment, and art.

The equipment he needed was simple: a workbench with saw frame, a small gas furnace, tools for cutting, drawing, scribing, and hammers. All of this was housed in a small shed attached to a scrap-metal yard. The yard and the shed were owned by an old friend of Martin's called Del Morrisey. And Del allowed him to use whatever gas or electricity he needed without charge. This was *his* investment because the jewel-maker regularly made him a gift of any item he liked. What Martin did not know was that Del accumulated a collection of pieces then, on his frequent trips to London, sold them at great profit to himself. And this one-sided business was expanding. European, and in particular French, dealers were showing great interest in the work and wanted to negotiate with the artist directly. All were quite enraptured by the originality and beauty of the *cloisonné* and *plique-à-jour* items they'd seen. That posed difficulties for his 'agent'. Del would have to tell Martin what he'd been up to and still retain the services of the young man who'd found a way to turn base metal into gold – or, at least, glass into a great deal of money.

Before that confrontation, however, there occurred the event which placed Martin far out of reach of dealers, friends and family alike. It was the event which, in metaphysics, is called 'fusion to unity' – though not in England where all of metaphysics is reduced to a matter of words; and even observable phenomena become noumenona. But this was far from a matter of words, and changed the young man's life – as I'd known it change other men's lives. Similar events are well documented by explorers, mountaineers, yachtsmen sailing long distances single-handed and, of course, the condition is one actively sought in Buddhism.

'I was in the workshop,' Martin told me. 'There's a window looks out on the lane but I was concentrating on a copper disc. It was for a *champlevé* pendant. I'd already scribed the design and I was starting to carve the channels. I had a lamp close-focussed on that. It's a job that needs an awful lot of concentration.'

'Was there anyone with you?'

'No, no. I can't work if I'm watched. Anyway – there was the small area of light and the brightness on the edge of the chisel and it was biting into the warm-coloured copper.'

'Do you hold your breath during the cut?'

Martin thought for a moment, then seemed pleased to discover something he'd not realised before. He smiled. 'Yes. That's right. I do. Or, I did – watching the thin sliver of metal curling up like a petal unfolding. While it's happening, it seems nothing else in the world is happening. There *is* nothing else in the world but that narrow, keen edge paring under layers of skin. And then it happened. Between my eyes, and my fingers holding the chisel, and the chisel, and the copper there was no division at all. There was no difference at all. It was all the same stuff. The same body. I flowed into the copper and the copper flowed into me. All the false dividing barriers just seemed to melt away.' He sprawled back in the passenger seat of my car and sighed. 'Can you understand that at all?'

'Yes. I can understand that perfectly. How long did the moment last?'

'I don't know. But I didn't want to break it. You've no idea how wonderful it felt. When I did look up I was looking out of the window and there was a newspaper boy on his morning round. He often came down the lane. It was a short cut for him. The thing was, I could hear him whistling. I knew his whistle. But though it was broad daylight I could hardly see him at all. What I could see...' Martin wet his lips. 'About *all* I could see was a small copper flame as he went flickering past the window.'

'Where?'

'Mm?' Martin was loth to drag his attention away from that vividly remembered sight.

'Where, in his body, was the flame?'

'Where it is in everyone. If it is there at all.'

'In me, where is it?

Martin stretched over and with palm inward and fingers extended he touched the centre of my chest at the solar plexus. 'There.' he said, then withdrew his fingers quickly and added, 'But you have a bright filament running up to your left shoulder. That's odd.'

'Not really. I have a scar on my left shoulder.'

When Martin went out to keep his appointment with Del Morrisey he felt bewildered in the street. It was like walking through a candle-lit procession in which the bearers of the candles were absent. He kept bumping into people because he wasn't making allowance for the bulk of the bodies which *they* knew they possessed. It was only with a conscious effort he was able to fill the outlines where he remembered they should be.

Before he reached Morrisey's house he was getting much better at such artificial perception. The scrap dealer greeted him effusively. He was big and warm and welcoming. But Martin stared at him in disbelief. There was *only* the outline. There was *only* the shadow. There was not even the slightest glimmer of a flame. Still, the jewel-maker went mechanically through the actions of

36

walking along the hallway in the wake of this dark ghost. He sat down and appeared to listen to the words the man spoke, but could hear only a rumbling noise.

For his part, Del Morrisey put on a good show and concocted a story to suit the business opportunities he now wished to exploit. He said that on his last visit to London he'd happened to meet a man who was in the jewellery trade and, as he just happened to have one of Martin's pieces with him, he showed it to the dealer. The dealer was interested and gave him his card. Del produced the card and crossed the room to hand it to Martin. But the young man saw only the shadow increasing and about to engulf him. He drew back in the chair. Del, as though anxious to plant the evidence of good intent, thrust the card into the pocket of Martin's jacket and went on with his spiel.

The young man in the chair felt an increasing sense of dread. He realised the reason why he couldn't hear the words was because they were coming from something which shouldn't be able to speak; as though an ambulatory carcase was talking. And still the rumbling noise went obscenely on and the corpse moved and believed itself to be alive. The feeling of revulsion grew too strong to be borne. Martin struggled to his feet and rushed from the room and the house. In that state of mind it was not surprising that he did not want to see Kate or Richard or his mother. There was the terrible fear that one of them would now be revealed in the same condition as Del Morrisey. As far as the jewel-maker was concerned he had killed Morrisey by *seeing* that he was dead. The barrier which had been erected between the former friends was as complete as that. He could not face the responsibility thus to kill the people he loved.

He had to get away. But first he went back to the workshop. When he looked at the bench and in the trays where the finished pieces were, he noticed what he'd never noticed before. They glowed. Dimly, but they glowed. Everything he'd lovingly made had part of him in it. In the car, as we drove towards Dun Laoghaire, it seemed obvious to me that he'd only been seeing more vividly what connoisseurs always see in a work of art. It is *that* which sets an original apart from the most expert copy.

In his workshop, the jewel-maker gathered all the finished pieces of jewellery into two plastic bags. When he reached the city centre again he just gave the fruits of his work away. The items which dealers in London and Paris had vied for were handed to startled pedestrians. Many refused to accept as a gift what they'd have paid through the nose for in Grafton Street. They knew anyone as generous as that would have to be a thief, and they couldn't entertain a thief in public. Eventually, though, everything was disposed of and Martin crossed the Liffey to the north side and the Terminal.

But now the strain of his new condition began to tell on his unprepared body. Several hours of super-alertness and a whole flood of strange and vivid perceptions overtaxed the more mundane faculties of balance and muscular co-ordination. Eventually he would learn to cope with all that, to select what should claim his attention and discriminate by an act of will, but in that first flood his body was left drifting and collapsed. *It* would not let him go on, and something else knew he should not. Not yet.

When I brought the car to a halt outside the end house of the terrace, Richard got out first to reconnoitre. He wanted to prepare his mother for the alarming sight of her younger son. The care was unnecessary. Beatrice was out. We carried Martin round the back and into the kitchen. Only when the patient was safely deposited in a chair did Richard trust himself to address Martin. 'Just as well she's out. Look at the state of you! And ye've left a bloody track on the path there like the road to Calvary.'

'They don't hurt. Just scratches.'

'Scratches! Look at them, ya mad bastard. Blood poisonin' for sure! It's lead paint on the girders, y'know. And splinters of rust and steel scale. My God, what a mess. She'd have a fit.' He unbuckled the fastening at the wrists of his overalls and rolled up his sleeves.

Martin said, 'If you never wore boots you could climb better – once the skin hardened.'

'Mad!' exclaimed Richard and gave me a look of supplication as he clattered a large metal basin into the sink and started filling it with water.

'You could use your toes.'

'Or take on bloody apes. Here!' He placed the basin on the tiled floor by Martin's torn feet. 'Where the blazes does she keep the soda?'

'It'll be under the sink with the sheep-dip. She doesn't trust hair-dressers either.'

Richard emptied a fair quantity of soda into the basin and stirred it impatiently with his hand. 'There! Get your feet into that.'

'No. I'd rather have scarred feet than burnt stumps.'

'You're sure you haven't touched a drop?'

'Everybody thinks I'm drunk. It must be the only way to live,' Martin said, then rocked back as Richard grabbed his ankles and plunged his feet into the water. 'Ooooh! Too much soda.'

'You'll need all of that to kill the poison.'

Martin tried to withdraw his feet, but Richard held them in and, since he was already on his knees, started bathing them.

Once the initial shock of the water was over Martin asked, 'If I was drunk, could I climb all that way up to see you? And would I?'

'You wouldn't, unless you were bent on suicide.'

'How high did I stand at the top there?'

'That wasn't the top. I stopped you at the thirty-meter sling.' Suddenly Richard became aware that I was watching him bathe his brother's feet and he turned to me with some embarrassment. 'Thanks very much, Mr...'

'Murray.'

'Mr Murray. We don't want to keep you.'

'Yes, we do!' Martin announced. 'I'd like you to stay.'

His brother was puzzled. 'D'ya know the man?'

'I do, now,' Martin said. Then directly to me, 'You saw me up there. Thirty meters on sheer steel. I'd no idea how the air rushes up. How everything sways and the world spins from under you.' He glanced down at the top of Richard's bent head. 'That's enough. I can do it.'

'You're right. There was more blood than injury.'

'They smart a bit, but that's all. It's too late for you to go back, isn't it? Today? I had to see you.'

'You didn't need to climb up to see me. I would have been down for my chit.'

'Oh, I didn't know you came down to eat.'

'Holy God! D'ya think I'd brew a can up there?' Richard got to his feet and, in doing so, noted the blood and gashes on his brother's arms. He yanked the shirt off his shoulders to reveal more abrasions. 'You're covered in muck! Come on. Before she gets back. A bath.' He grabbed Martin's arm and dragged him towards the stair.

Martin protested in some alarm, 'You are *not* going to bath me!'

'I am not. Ye can fend for yourself.' As he bundled the younger brother upstairs some of his anger returned. 'In fact once you're in it ya can drown if it'll please you.'

I heard the bathroom door slam shut and Richard clattered downstairs again. He jerked his thumb over his shoulder and informed me with heavy sarcasm, 'That's what education does for you.' He at once set about emptying and cleaning the basin then drying the floor.

I disagreed. 'No. There's no education goes as far as that.'

'Well, thank God I had none of it, anyway. Would ya like a dish o' tea?'

'Thank you.'

He filled the kettle. 'Are *you* a scholar, Mr Murray?'

By this he meant a university graduate. 'No. I'm a jobbing playwright.'

His eyes widened. 'Surely you'd have to go to a university for that!'

'Many people think so. But all you really need for it is the talent.'

As he tested the efficiency of the electric kettle with the palm of his hand, his thoughtful expression indicated he might want to pursue the subject. It was of little interest to me, however, as long as I could learn more about these ill-matched brothers. The tea-making and the drinking of it gave me the opportunity to question the burly steel erector and to extract a great deal of information about the Doyle family.

They were born deep in Mayo where Beatrice was in domestic service. Their father was a Dublin man who was regularly out that way for the summer work. In the autumn of each year he went back to Dublin. But the year after Martin was born he gave up his country excursions altogether. There was no doubt in Richard's mind now that he also intended to give up his wife and family. The man reckoned without the fortitude of Beatrice. She quit her job, packed what little she had of her own and, with Richard just able to walk, carried Martin in her arms across the whole island and into the city. To her, the family unit was a sacred entity and Doyle would have to learn that it could never be escaped.

Yet, he escaped it – in prison. Johnnie Doyle was a professional thief. The summer sabbaticals had been a ruse to throw the Garda off his scent and let the dust settle. Eventually, his previous convictions exhausted the patience of the courts and he was sent away for a long time. The family didn't find out when he was released because he never came back to them.

The desertion was overcome by the mother's hard work, and all hope was pinned on Martin. He was the bright one. He was the son who'd make up for the father. He was the symbol whose success would repay all the sacrifices that were made for his education. In his reference to those years, Richard could not disguise the fact that he'd spent most of his life in the shadow of his younger brother. It came out as pride, or resentment, or affection – but it was always there.

We heard the bathroom door open but Martin did not come downstairs. Richard paused in rinsing the mugs, then banged his open hand on the draining tray. 'The bugger!' He lunged towards the stair. 'I forgot the bloody roof.'

I followed him upstairs at a more leisurely pace. Martin was in the bedroom putting on his clothes and Richard stood sentinel at the window. The escape route he'd remembered was through that window and onto the wash-house roof, from which it was a simple drop to the ground. Martin looked up when I came into the room and smiled. 'You're curious now, aren't you?'

41

'Yes. I'd like to know why you climbed up through the girders.'

'I wanted to see Richard.'

'What's wrong wi' comin' to the house when I'm there?'

'Your wife is there, too. And we know she can't stick me for five minutes.'

'That's not true.' Richard grinned. 'But *ten* minutes would be pushin' it.'

'I want to explain – before Beattie gets back.'

'Oh! Before Beattie gets back' — Richard fumbled inside his shirt and produced the bundle of letters — 'you'd better put these in a safer place.'

Martin gave a quick and knowing look at his burgled bag before he moved to the window and took the package. 'Well – however you got them, I'm glad you know I was taking them with me.' He pushed the letters into his hip pocket.

'You're not goin' anywhere.'

'I helped you then, and you will help me now – for your own sake.'

'Since when do I do what you tell me?' demanded Richard.

'Since you were eight until you wrote those letters.'

'That's a bloody rotten trick…'

'Isn't it true?'

'… castin' that up.'

'Reminding.'

'A bloody rotten trick.' Richard made a half-concealed angry gesture in my direction.

Martin didn't follow the gesture but kept staring at his brother's face with an avid solicitude. And then I saw the idea occur to him – though I had no inkling of its importance at that moment. With great deliberation he handed the letters back to Richard. 'Take them. Destroy them if you like and I'll forget I ever read them.'

Richard's first instinct was to snatch at the chance but he hesitated. 'I wrote them to you. They're yours.'

'Nothing is mine any more,' Martin said.

After a long pause Richard extended his hand and took the bundle of paper. His relief was evident as he concealed them again inside his shirt.

Martin changed the subject. 'Mr Murray, what do you think of this room?'

'What I think of the room is not important. I'd really...'

'It's important to us,' Martin interrupted. He turned to his brother. 'Isn't it Richard? What would you say is remarkable about this room?'

'It looks exactly the same to me,' Richard said.

'Right. And why? Who has kept it so?'

'Beattie, of course.'

'None other. And why? Not for herself. She can hardly shake a broom in this place once a year by the look of it. Not for herself. She has kept it waiting for me. You won't come back so your bed has gone. But I'm still at large. Not married. So she's keeping a home for me that I don't want. Beattie herself would rather be with you and the children.'

Richard said, 'We've asked her often enough. She likes it here.'

'Oh, you are stupid! How could anybody like it *here*?'

'She refuses to leave her neighbours and friends.'

'Don't believe her! Is that too much to ask? Don't be*lieve* her.'

There was no question in my mind that Martin was right. Beatrice, having been deserted by a husband and having spent years in a constant struggle to pay the rent and hold a family together, must look on this drab little house as the only evidence that her life had been worthwhile. There should always be a home for Martin to come back to. Perhaps, also, she had hopes that her husband would, at long last, return.

It occured to me that Martin's experience of the fusion to unity had done a great deal more for him than make visible the human spirit. He'd gained an astonishing grasp of human frailty as well; in particular, the blind adherence with which pride can defeat love, while masquerading as love. Yet, still, they would not let him go. He must have known there would be a hard struggle in prospect. That was why he'd insisted I should stay. Without my being quite aware of it, I had been recruited as Martin's ally. I asked, 'Where was your bed, Richard?'

'On the other side, there, against the wall.' He indicated the corner where the book-case now stood and the wall under the window. 'We had the cupboard between us.' His attention was caught by something on top of the cupboard and reached up to grasp it.

Martin laughed. 'The telephone!'

Richard handed the instrument to me. 'Did *you* ever have them?'

I examined the two tin cans. They were joined together by a long piece of wire; threaded into a hole in the base and knotted inside. 'No. How does it work?'

Richard grinned. 'It *doesn't* work. I'll show ya.' He unwound the wire and threw one of the cans to Martin who caught it. 'You speak first.'

Martin put the open end of the can to his mouth while Richard retreated through the open door onto the landing to tighten the wire. He put *his* can to his ear. Martin said, 'Hello! Hello! Richard?' then switched to 'receive'.

Richard replied, 'Yes. I can hear you.'

Martin smiled up at me. 'You see? I can hear him.'

'But so can I.'

'Sure. But when there was only the two of us it was easy to believe we couldn't hear *without* the can.' He applied it once more to his mouth. 'Come in, spiderman, your time is up.'

Richard promptly reappeared as though to vindicate the usefulness of the device. As he rewound the wire he said, 'The important thing to know is, who's supposed to be talking and who's supposed to be listening.' He opened the cupboard and tossed the cans inside. 'That bugger always wanted t'be talkin'.' Martin nodded in amused agreement that this was true. He threw himself on the bed to lie full-length on his back while Richard continued to rummage in the cupboard. 'I wonder what in hell happened to my stilts.'

'Your *stilt*,' Martin corrected.

I laughed. 'Surely nothing can be done with one stilt!'

Richard gave me an indignant look. 'I could *hop* on it.'

'Little did he know,' Martin mused, 'he was inventing the pogo stick.'

'It was a fine stilt,' Richard assured us as he pulled something else from the cupboard. It was like a bolt of linen but unrolled to reveal an acupuncture chart.

44

'That's mine,' Martin said.

'Fine I know! Didn't you try it on me. Gave me a sore on the calf o' m'leg wouldn't heal for weeks.'

Martin shrugged contentedly. 'I was using the wrong kind of needle.'

'A bloody darnin' needle it was!'

I asked Richard, 'What age were you then?'

'Oh, that was ...' he referred to his brother, 'when was it?'

'Well *you* must have been around fourteen – remember?'

Richard nodded happily. 'That's *right*. Oh yes, I do.' He turned to me. 'He was always lookin' for cures. A magic way o' doin' everything.'

Martin commented, 'I still am.'

But Richard was preoccupied with his affectionate memories of that time and told me, 'We used to have telepathy experiments...' There was a muffled gurgle from the bed, '... that landed me with flu. I'll tell ya, it was me had to crouch outside the window there, on the wash-house roof – in the dead of night this was – thinkin' of words, while he sat in here notin' whatever came into me mind.'

I asked, 'And was he any good at it?'

'Oh, he was a marvel at it. Eighty percent right. Got practically every word I was thinkin' – like: warmth, sleep, bed, cats. A marvel in telepathy. Damn all use with the needle, though.'

'What was he trying to cure you of?' I asked. 'With the needle?'

'VD.' Martin piped up from the bed.

I gasped, 'At fourteen?'

The brothers looked at each other and laughed in unison. Martin explained, 'He *claimed* it was V.D. It turned out that what was worrying him was the full fruit of puberty.'

Richard threw the acupuncture chart back into the cupboard. 'Whatever it was, the darnin' needle did no good at all.'

In the silence, both brothers continued to smile at the recollection of themselves in that unchanged little room; the feeling of warmth and affection was almost tangible.

45

To my surprise, I was conscious for the first time of resentment that I had not had a brother when I was young. Of course, I never had one at all, but lacking such a necessity when I was young now seemed an unjust deprivation.

The atmosphere in the bedroom from which neither youth, nor love, nor junk had been allowed to escape was interrupted. Kate returned. She'd been back to their flat and had spent a long time trying to get through on the telephone to a London number. We heard her calling as she let herself in. 'Mrs Doyle. Mrs Doyle, are you there?'

Richard went out on the landing and shouted, 'We're up here!'

When she saw Martin sitting placidly on the blankets her face lit up with obvious relief.

Richard said, 'I thought you'd be round earlier.'

'I was.'

'Oh yes, she was,' Martin confirmed. 'And took it very well.' He smiled as he extended his hand towards her.

Kate went to him and placed the business card in his outstretched palm. 'This is yours. Your mother gave it to me.'

Martin looked at the card. 'No. It's not mine.' He obviously had no recollection of Del Morrisey thrusting it into his pocket, but the denial seemed to Kate yet another subterfuge.

The girl glanced at me. 'Are you the doctor?'

Martin chuckled. 'No. He's the scarlet pimpernel. What about this card?'

Kate said, 'It belongs to a jewel dealer in London. I asked him if he knew where you were or if he was expecting you. He told me he'd never even heard of you.'

I asked, 'Did you mention that Martin makes jewels?'

Kate was impatient. 'No. What difference would that make?'

'All the difference in the world to a jewel dealer.'

'I wasn't trying to sell him jewels. I was trying to find Martin, or find out what had made him ...' She stopped abruptly. This was her business and she'd no intention of sharing it with a stranger. Indeed, she had no intention of prolonging a painful and baffling situation. Now that she

46

knew he was at home and not injured there seemed nothing for it but to accept his decision that their relationship was over. This was *the day*.

Martin hadn't taken his eyes off her face since she came in and he knew her well enough to realise there would be no more argument. He said, 'This box of a room is too bloody crowded with four in it. Richard, will you make our guest a bit more comfortable?'

We went downstairs, but this time to the front room. There wasn't much light, even in the middle of the afternoon, because the window was practically blanked out with a complex arrangement of mock-lace curtains and screens. It was a window no casual passer-by, or even dedicated peeping Tom, could pierce. Nor did the decor improve matters. All that had once been bright had darkened with age. Richard and I sat in deep, musty armchairs. Kate's being there had quite broken the spell of happy nostalgia and the older brother was reminded of why they were keeping watch on Martin. After a long silence in which I sensed a baffled anger rising, he blurted the question, 'Can *you* understand this?'

'I think so.'

'Then tell me. For God's sake tell me why it has to change. We're all happy enough. Why does *he* have to change?'

'Perhaps he had no choice.'

'And he gives us no choice. Is that fair?'

'You have your wife and family.'

'Sure. And I have a brother. The *brother* I had, before I had a thing else.' His square, weatherbeaten face was being held in a strong pose but his voice betrayed a lack of control. 'I could always depend on that, no matter what. When I was … sick … it was him I counted on.'

'You seem a healthy man now.'

'Oh, I've been healthy since … since then.' He sighed and his breath seemed to pass over several bumps on its way out.

'What was the trouble? Then?'

'Ach, it was nerves, I think. A kind of nervous breakdown. And a God-awful depression that had me near endin' m'self.'

47

'And how did Martin help? I asked.

'He wouldn't come home. He was in England, y'see, at the university. It was just before I got married.'

'So *you* were about to leave home?' He nodded, but apparently did not see the relevance. The memory of the event claimed all his attention as he hunched forward in the chair. And it was, I knew, a crucial event; much more crucial for the rural Irish than the city English can imagine. And the Doyles were rural Irish though they'd come to Dublin. Beatrice had imparted to her sons what had been bred in her. It was not a conscious principle which had to be remembered. It was much, much deeper and couldn't be forgotten.

Indeed all Celts possess an atavistic urge to preserve the unity of the family. And it is stronger in a poor family; where it seems likely the most they will ever have is each other. They may curse it or fight against it, but the bond remains. 'You wrote to Martin?'

Richard nodded. 'From the hospital. Oh, they were terrible letters I wrote. I was sick and broken or I'd never have wrote such things.'

'What things?'

He raised his hand to support his forehead – and also to conceal his eyes from me. 'Warped, vicious things about my father. And my mother. And Ruth, too, though she was the girl I was goin' to marry. Everything seemed so ... *black*. I needed to hit out at everything that had changed or was changin'. And I laid hold of the one certain thing in my life – and that was Martin.'

'But how did he help?'

Richard rubbed his brow. 'He stayed out of reach. Time and again I threatened to kill m'self unless he came home. But he knew I wouldn't do it with him away.' He sighed more deeply and slumped back in the chair, still with a protective hand on his forehead. 'Some of the other things I wrote, though. Cruel, vicious things. And I remember doing it. I remember the panic of rage I was in at the sheer bloody *effort* of writin'. But it was worth it. Every time the letter was written and I gave it to the nurse to post... Each time I'd lay back in the bed exhausted, but glad. I knew it was evil but I was glad that I'd managed to smuggle another live bit of me out beyond the reach of anyone.' He fumbled for a cigarette and lit it without looking at me. 'I lay back in the bed with every muscle shakin'. And yet I was smilin', while the tears gushed out o' me eyes in a constant stream.'

Neither of us spoke again until he'd finished the cigarette and I reflected that when Martin handed back the wad of letters he'd returned a fully paid-up ransom. And I was struck by Richard's assertion that Martin had helped him through the nervous collapse by *not* being there. By *not* coming home. He kept Richard safe by being at a distance and thus no part of the conspiracy the sick man felt he must fight. We were interrupted by the arrival of Beatrice, and the sick man – long since cured – shouted, 'Where the hell have *you* been?'

'At the shops. Where else!'

'With nature boy deranged up there?'

Her cool stare flickered. 'He's back then?' It amazed me that the woman could exhibit such control over her feelings. What had once been necessary to shield the children from fear had now become a proud habit.

Richard indicated me. 'Mr Murray brought him back. Brought us both back.'

She gave me a brief but comprehensive look. 'I see.' She turned to Richard again as she untied her headscarf. 'What about you, though? Missin' a shift.'

'What about you? Out at the shops, b'God!'

Beatrice sniffed. 'The world'll not stop for one man desertin' it. We've still got to eat, y'know.'

'Kate's here too. She's up there with him.'

'*Is* she, now. Well, what a great pity I was out at all, with a good chance of a card school goin' here.' As she hefted her shopping bag she addressed me. 'You'll stay for your tea, Mister?'

'Thank you.'

Beatrice went into the kitchen and shortly thereafter we heard Kate descending the stair, alone. Richard called to her and she paused at the door of the front room. He asked if she'd drop him off at the building site so that he could collect his car and she agreed. She also spoke to me and wished me success with the play. I invited her to

49

come and see it as my guest and she said she would. All this was no more than a polite gloss over the real event which was not being mentioned. Kate had just said good-bye to the man she loved and knew she would not see him again.

I was left alone in that depressing room preserved for unwelcome visitors. Upstairs, Martin remained still gathered for flight but no doubt sensible of the pain he was causing. At the back of the house, in the kitchen, his mother was clashing pans and rattling utensils with angry vigour as she prepared the meal. It came to me that we were all strangers now, though two of us were mother and son. And there was no point in my feeling irritation at the unnecessary difficulty of the situation. Such difficulties seem unnecessary only in *other* people's lives and so can be reported as unreal by outsiders. However, I was an outsider who had interfered, and what I did require, if I were going to put the experience to use, was an explanation. Martin, I felt, owed me an explanation and I marched upstairs to demand it.

He was squatting in front of the bookcase, reading. My abrupt and rather breathless arrival did not startle him. 'Ah! The changing of the guard, is it?'

That seemed to me a callous remark but I had to concede it was apt. The young man had been under almost constant surveillance for close on thirty-six hours – most of them in that small room. And his lack of moping or pity allowed me to be brisk about what I'd made my business. 'I'd like you to tell me why you are doing this.'

'Sit down,' he said, and indicated the sagging bed. 'And first, tell *me* if you are going to drive me away from this house when we've eaten.'

'Drive you where?'

'To Dun Laoghaire. I'll get a boat from there.'

'Very well. Now, why?' I insisted.

'I thought you understood.'

'The fusion to unity, I understand. The fear of finding a death of spirit, I understand. But you must have been reassured about Kate and Richard and your mother as soon as you saw them again – so why must you still get away?'

He sighed and laid the book open on the stained rug. 'Because that is not all I see. There's more to it than a mere presence or absence of spirit. There's its freedom to grow.'

'Yours, you mean?'

'No. Theirs. Theirs first, then mine. Theirs is stifled because of me. I'd never have realised that, as I was before.' His voice, as he continued, betrayed no overtones of sadness. Instead, there was warmth and a very practical compassion. 'I must go where I can be of use.' He sat at ease with legs crossed on the floor as he talked. 'Kate, Richard, Beatrice – I'm no longer any use to them. All we need from each other we already have. Going on as we were ... it would just be a matter of re-living, instead of living for the first time every day.' He smiled as though to admit that the re-living might have its satisfactions. But that was not enough.

'How do plan to be of use?' I asked.

'By going where I am needed for the *first* time. By offering what abilities I have in the lives of strangers.'

'Why strangers?'

'Always strangers,' he said. 'I can love and care for them without obliging them to love or care for me in return.' He sucked in his breath as though he felt a stab of pain. 'I am sick of *barter*.'

I asked him, 'Why should they ask your help if they *can't* love you in return.'

Martin smiled. 'They accept gifts, don't they? I'll be a useful gift. I fear no one because I am no threat to any. I hate no one because I have been loved. I envy no one because my whole purpose is to make them seem enviable to me. What more could they fail to ask for – and get?'

I had to admire the sheer efficiency of the concept, and the beauty of it, too. 'Yes. That would be worth doing if it didn't mean destroying what you have here.'

Martin shook his head and repeated, 'What I had here is over. For Richard and me, the time was to be boys and brothers. We have been that. For Beatrice, my time was as a child; and I have been that. For Kate, a lover; and I have been that.' He got to his feet impatiently. 'But what are we to be next, if I stay?' He turned to the window. 'I have already done what was expected of me and gave what I

51

could. The pain is, that I was also given what I cannot return. To take any more would be robbery.' He stood at the window with his back to me and looked down at the cracked paving stones of the garden path and the wrecked wooden gate supported by one hinge. 'No. It's over. What I was to Richard and my mother and Kate, I can never be again. All I'm taking from them is a reminder of a memory.' He turned to me and asked with great earnestness, 'Surely they will let me take that, and go?'

And, eventually, they did. There were only three of us at the kitchen table for the meal Beatrice had prepared, then shared with Martin and me. Richard didn't come back although we waited for him. But his mother quite understood his absence. 'It must have been too late in the day,' she said. 'And his wife will have his own dinner prepared.' Clearly, a dinner prepared by a wife for her husband took precedence over most things. But my own feeling was that Richard could not face saying good-bye.

Nor, in the remaining time Martin spent in her house, did Beatrice say anything to dissuade him from going. There was her pride to consider and Martin allowed her to maintain that last defence. When the meal was over, I went out and waited in the car for him. On the journey to the harbour I asked if he yet knew why his first attempt had been thwarted.

'Yes,' he said. 'I think so. They had to know that, whatever became of me, it was my decision. But more important, that none of them was to blame.' I was aware of him smiling in the passing lights of other cars. 'It was a matter of courtesy, really, that I'd overlooked.'

The play at the Eblana did go well and Kate did come to see it. We had a long talk in the bar of my hotel afterwards and it was then she told me of her attempt to dissuade Martin. But she was already building up defences and before she left there was the clearly implied suggestion that Martin would not have gone through with his crazy idea if I hadn't encouraged him, then provided him with an easy means of escape. She did not really believe that, but I did not deny it, so we parted amicably enough.

Richard brought his wife to see a performance. His wife confided to me that she, at least, was glad the younger brother had packed his bags. Rather sharply she told me, 'Now I need hear no more from him what Martin says or what Martin advises him to do.' By 'him' she meant her husband. Apparently, he had plans to start his own business but Martin had repeatedly advised him against it. Richard, who'd been getting the drinks, rejoined us before I could question her further on that point of friction. Still, it was refreshing to find someone who approved of my complicity in letting Martin get away.

But the pattern of all this refused to become clear. Nevertheless, I put my notes in order and started work on the mechanics of staging the crisis I'd observed at first hand. That vigil in an upper room in Dublin seemed perfect material for a future festival, and yet I had doubts. Wasn't it all too *strange*? Too bizarre? Wasn't there a danger that Martin would come out of it as too self-centred and callous, no matter how accurately I reported the purpose of his priestlike task? I put the material away and worked on other things.

It was Martin himself who reassured me enough to get the play written. Almost a year after the events I've been describing, a small package was delivered to my flat in London. It got there by way of a theatre and then my agent. There was no card or letter with it but the object itself left no doubt about the sender. It was a silver tie-clasp ornamented with a small, beautifully worked *cloisonné* enamelled flower. The tiny petals were scarlet and it seemed likely the flower was a pimpernel. I have it still.

It was not until three or four years had passed that I was working in Dublin again. And, again, it was at the Eblana during the theatre festival, run with inexhaustible optimism and flair by Brendan Smith.

One of my first visitors was Kate. And she came with her husband. And they talked about their children. When I managed to steer them away from that enthralling subject, I asked about Richard and his mother. Apparently he had recently started up his own hardware business, which was thriving. His mother, of course, lived with Richard and her grandchildren at Killiney. They adored her and she doted on them. 'Of course,' I said, and reflected how ironic it was that Beattie's opportunity 'to get out of the gutter' as she put it, had been granted by Richard and not Martin – in whom she'd placed all her hopes.

I could not help noticing that Kate was puzzled at my interest in the family. It was as though she'd forgotten how this state of affairs had come about. When introducing me to her husband she'd added, 'I met Mr Murray after his last play in Dublin.' There was no mention at all of the events before that. Fearing Richard might also be blessed with such a lapse of memory, I made no effort to contact him. But I did take a run out to where that little terraced house once stood in Kilmainham. Something else had already been built there.

So – all there was to show for Martin's passing was a beautiful tie-clasp and several happy lives.

There should be more such jewel-makers.

The Previous Tenant

Since I've no property of my own, a lot of my life has been spent in hotel rooms or furnished flats. The hotels are much the same anywhere and the flats don't vary a great deal. Only this I know: if there's musak in the lobby the accommodation won't be warm enough in winter.

On one of the occasions when I had work in London, the writing and rehearsal schedule dictated remaining there throughout the winter. But the quiet little hotel in Hampstead which I'd chosen was not very keen on guests who did more than sleep in their rooms. Since they had not warned me it was a *wagon-lit* establishment I complained to the management and rather pointedly wondered if my room was secretly double-booked to a night-shift worker. But the manager wouldn't be drawn on the issue and I started to search for a furnished flat.

I was lucky. The actress, Barbara Cree, mentioned that one would shortly fall vacant in the block where she lived. Since I was visiting her at the time, I knew there was no musak and the diameter of the central heating pipes seemed more than adequate. The porter assured me of his intercession on my behalf and I moved into the place on Lower Sloane Street only a couple of days after the previous tenant moved out.

It was an area with which I was not very familiar. To me Sloane Square meant only the Royal Court theatre, where I'd had some business a couple of years earlier for a production of *Bright Scene Fading*. The flat was on the seventh floor and looked out along Turks Row and the grounds of the Royal Hospital. Whereas I was pleased that

55

I would not be staring into somebody else's windows, I regretted the volume of traffic roaring down to the embankment and Chelsea Bridge. On the whole, though, I was very pleased with myself that I'd found a place to work and that I'd been able to move in so quickly.

If I'd known about the strange circumstances I was soon to discover I would have made a point of meeting the previous tenant before he left. His name, according to the buzzer panel at the entrance, was Vernon Slater. His chief claim to interest, according to the porter's wife, was that he'd lived in the flat a long time – much longer than anyone else then resident – and his departure was very sudden.

'Where has he gone?' I asked her.

'Lewes,' she said. 'In Sussex. At least that's the address he left with us.'

I nodded and let myself out of the lift we were sharing. There was something rather odd in Mrs Dobbie's remark about the address. It was as though she doubted if Mr Slater had *really* gone to Sussex. Of course, she and her husband had been put to extra work by the need, suddenly, to prepare the flat for me at short notice. That must have been irritating. Everything had to be cleaned or polished and anything faulty repaired to give the impression nobody had ever lived there before.

The suddenness of the previous tenant's departure and my urgent need to move in must have provided the property managers with a welcome bonus. It was at the end of the first week in November I arrived. But the rent was payable in advance on the *first* of each month. Since it was unlikely the managers would consider a rebate, that meant the previous tenant had been prepared to waive about three quarters of the sum he'd already paid. He must have been very anxious to get away from London for, in addition to the basic rent, there were estimated heating and lighting charges levied monthly in advance. He'd virtually made a gift of those to me.

In the flat, I looked around for some evidence of the long-time occupant. The man was beginning to interest me. But Mr and Mrs Dobbie had done a very thorough job in clearing out all the drawers and cupboards. And

56

however Slater had things arranged, they had rearranged it to the standard layout. The furnishings were variations of the Habitat in Barbara Cree's flat a couple of floors below. The beige walls and apricot woodwork were fresh and bright. There was no sign that the supplied paintings covered spaces where a personal choice had hung. There were no cigarette burns on the carpet or stains on the upholstery. Apparently, Mr Slater had been a model tenant as far as the fabric was concerned. I tested the lights and only then noticed the ceiling. It had been finished in gloss white paint and it had not been cleaned prior to my arrival. Time had been short and there was no need. The ceiling was not dirty. However, in the artificial light, there was a broad, matt patch which glittered. It was as though that patch above the couch had been painted with a very fine crystalline powder.

At the next suitable opportunity I tried to get more information from the porter's wife. I asked her, 'Was Mr Slater an elderly man?'

She gave me a rather worried look. 'You mean the previous tenant?'

I nodded. 'Yes.' But then it occured to me that she hadn't told me his name. I'd seen that at the entrance before the little card was removed. I'd breached some protocol by referring to him by name so I rephrased the question. 'Was the previous tenant an elderly man?'

'No. Not elderly. Not a *young* man, but not elderly.'

'Middle-aged, then. About my age?'

She did not look at me as she continued to swab the tiled floor of the entrance hall. 'He was a good bit older than you, Mr Murray.'

We were, it seemed, talking about a middle-aged man well able to afford the penalties of obeying a sudden whim. I asked, 'What was his occupation?'

'He was in the civil service. As far as *we* knew.'

'And he lived alone?'

'Quite alone. There was no trouble with him about that.'

Again a throwaway remark which hinted at more than it stated. She could mean there was trouble with him about *other* things or there was *that* trouble with other people in the block.

She must have intended the latter because she went on to raise her eyebrows over that actress friend of mine and Mr Sandys who'd shared her flat. Now Mr Sandys was gone and she had another man there. I said I'd met him and his name was Bill Thompson. 'He seems a very pleasant, harmless kind of person,' I said.

'Yes. But what'll happen when Mr Sandys comes back?' Mrs Dobbie asked. No doubt she feared violent rows and broken dishes which would have to be replaced long after the items had gone out of stock in the shops. Servicing these flats was no joke.

You will think I had very little to do with my time if I started checking up on every previous tenant of accommodation I rented. In fact, I rarely did so because in most cases the evidence suggested that the person I replaced was a totally uninteresting slob. What was different on this occasion was that the previous tenant had taken great care *not* to leave evidence of his long sojourn in Lower Sloane Street. Like a drunk driver who proceeds with such exemplary caution he immediately prompts the traffic patrol to assume that anyone driving as soberly as that must be drunk, Vernon Slater gave the impression of being too good to be true. And whereas such people are no more my business than careless slobs, they excite my professional antennae. Also, the conviction that there was something *wrong* about Mr Slater was greatly strengthened by a fascinating discovery.

I was stacking my large cardboard boxes in the cupboard which housed the electricity meter and bumped against that fitting. Something dropped on the floor from behind the meter. It was a knitting needle; about six inches long, made of bone and very fine. I picked it up and went to the window to take a closer look. If I'd found it anywhere else but where it had fallen my inspection would have been brief and my conclusion would have been that it belonged to a long-gone female tenant of the flat.

But knitting with needles as fine as that would require a woman with very good eyesight and a great deal of

58

patience. There was less could be done with it by a man –
and only *one* needle, at that. I put on my reading glasses
and looked very closely at each tip. One end was cut
square and the other meticulously filed into a chisel shape.
No. Not chisel. Screwdriver.

Equipped with a flashlight I burrowed into the cupboard again. Below the dials the lead seals were intact as
was the little paper sticker which warned that tampering
with the device was dangerous. Below that, the wires
emerged from the common duct of the rising main. I
shone the torch all around the installation. The duct
continued above the meter. Since all the flats were
identical in layout, the main rose without deviation
through all the floors in the block. As far as I could see,
everything was as it should be. I was just about to back out
again on my hands and knees when my attention was
caught again by the red printed official sticker. It wasn't
sticking. I pressed it against the control plate and was
aware of what felt like a little blister. Curling the sticker
out of the way, I brought the torch closer to examine the
plate. It reflected a gleam of unpainted metal.

I smiled and scurried out for the knitting needle. It fitted
the tiny hole which had been drilled in the control plate.
With great care, I inserted this non-conducting screwdriver until it engaged the potential screw inside the
meter. I felt a very slight resistance to pressure then
turned the screw very slowly in an anti-clockwise direction. It took a great deal of concentration to keep the
needle at right-angles to the plate and a constant, though
delicate, pressure with so fine an instrument but
eventually I saw that the revolving disc in the dial of the
meter had stopped revolving. The flat was now supplied
with completely free power. I tested the lights in the
room, the wall sockets and the cooker in the kitchen
before reversing the procedure and returning my part of
the system to the charge of the LEB.

Filled with jubilant satisfaction, I threw myself full-
length on the couch and lit a cigarette to consider the
implications of my discovery. There is nothing remarkable
in wishing to defraud the public utilities. Many people try
to do it, though very few succeed. Yet here was a man

who did not need to do it and *did* succeed. The precision of his method was as remarkable as the fact that he did it at all. He could afford, and was willing, to throw money away on rent and charges yet went to a considerable amount of trouble to diddle the meter. There was only one explanation which would reconcile these conflicting actions and I was fairly sure I knew what that was.

My attention was caught once more by the ceiling directly above me. At this point I did not connect it with the other irregularities. It was merely puzzling and unusual. I shone the torch directly on the broad patch over the couch. It seemed to glitter even more brightly. I stood on the cushions but could not reach high enough to touch the powdery looking surface. There was a high stool in the kitchen and I fetched it. When I moved the couch back and stood on that I was able to rub my fingers on the ceiling. The coating looked and felt like salt, but it did not taste like salt. In fact it had a bitter metallic taste.

And one discovery led directly to another. As I was about to roll the couch back into position I could not help noticing the depressions in the carpet where the previous tenant must have had a different piece of furniture. The indentations matched those of a light sideboard which was now positioned against the opposite wall. But the marks in the carpet were far too deep, unless he'd stored something extremely heavy in the two long shallow drawers.

All this imposed a tantalising need to find out more about the man who had suddenly fled from London. I decided to ask my actress acquaintance downstairs, but waited until the afternoon when I was sure she'd be out of bed. In fact she was rather more than an acquaintance. I'd been commissioned to write a play for her. After a few conversational feints in that direction I got down to the more interesting business. 'Did you know Mr Slater?'

'Slater ... Slater...' She rolled the name around in her memory to see if it would drop into an existing hole. 'No, I don't think so.'

'I mean the man whose flat I now have.'

'Ah! The previous tenant.' Evidently Mrs Dobbie's

protocol was catching. 'Can't say I *knew* him. I spoke to him several times going out and coming in.'

'What was your impression of him?'

'He was tall and thin,' she began, then realised that could scarcely be the sort of impression I wanted. 'A married man. He liked music. Quite a few times when I was getting back from the theatre he'd just been to a concert. He was always alone. He wore old-fashioned-looking clothes – though they were good quality.'

'But what *sort* of man was he?' I asked, using the shorthand question – and inflection – which actors often use when facing a new role.

That got below the surface. She said, 'A bitter man, I would have thought. A man with a grudge. Very smoothly concealed, of course. But *thinly* concealed. I'd say it wouldn't take much for the jagged edges to poke through.' Barbara smiled. 'Is that enough?'

'A dangerous man, do you think?'

'Perhaps. When provoked.'

'What age?'

'About sixty,' Barbara said. 'But very alert, and sharp.'

'Excellent,' I said.

'Why are you so interested in him? He didn't leave a corpse up there, did he?'

'If he did, I haven't found it yet.'

'A bad smell, then?'

'More like that. In a way, there *is* a bad smell.'

She remembered something else. 'He must have done a lot of cooking.'

'What makes you think so?'

'Well, especially at week-ends. Often when I was walking towards the flats along Turks Row I noticed that his windows were all steamed up. And closed.'

Turks Row ran directly away from the flats' frontage and from there the whole building could be seen. I asked, 'Not just the kitchen window?'

'No, both. Kitchen and living room.' She repeated what was to her the odd circumstance. 'Steamed up and *closed*.'

We then went on to talk about matters of more general interest. I reported Mrs Dobbie's misgivings about the new man in Barbara's life.

The actress laughed. 'There's no danger of brawling at the moment. Bill's in Denmark until the end of the month. And after that we're going to get married.'

'Marriage does not preclude brawling,' I said.

She grinned mischievously. 'How would you know that?'

'I often stay with married friends.'

'They probably do it just to make you feel better. When Bill and I have our first brawl we'll invite you down.'

'Invite the Dobbies,' I said, 'they'd make better fielders.'

I went back up to my flat. Barbara had been a great help. Of course, most women can see the internal mechanism of people better than men, but actresses have cause to trust the ability and to express it. I wondered at the cause of Slater's bitterness and if his sudden departure was a sign that something had forced the jagged edges to show through.

Later that day the telephone rang. I sighed. It would be at least a week before the Post Office allotted me an ex-directory number, and it seemed only courteous to inform callers that Mr Slater had moved. But this wasn't a tradesman or a subscription hawker of *Time* magazine.

'Slater?' the man's voice said.

Still in the flush of my recent detective work, I said, 'Yes.'

'It hasn't arrived yet. And we want it back.' The caller had a very resonant English voice and apart from conveying impatience also conveyed authority.

'Oh?'

'We want you to bring it back and we'll give you until Friday. Got that? Friday. Latest!'

'It's not my fault,' I said, truthfully enough.

There was a marked pause on the other end of the line before the caller hung up. It seemed likely he knew what Slater sounded like on the phone and I didn't sound enough like Slater to pursue the conversation even one word further. But for a few seconds – after he hung up and before the line was disconnected – I heard a very distinctive tone which I thought I recognised. While the sound was still fresh in mind I called the recorded information tape which gives dialling tones for European

62

countries. It was as I had thought. The call to Slater had been placed in France.

Gradually the evidence was building up. Brief as the phone conversation had been it had provided a few gleaming nuggets. No doubt it is a by-product of my trade that I listen more acutely than most people. Whatever is said to me, my automatic response always monitors three distinct aspects. The first is to ask *why* it is being said to me, or at all. The second examines *how* it is being said. Coming a poor third is the only thing most other people hear – *what* is being said. I also note the length and intention of pauses which most people wait through rather than listen to.

Thus informed, it was certain that whatever the business between the caller and Slater it was secret or illegal. Any bona fide official or businessman would not have hung up when he found an impostor. He would have challenged me. As to the relationship, the manner and the words indicated that the caller employed Slater to perform some service or had paid for an item which Slater had failed to deliver – to France presumably.

Peripheral to all this was the fact that Slater was a civil servant and so there could be very few commodities he'd be in a position to sell. Moreover, he'd either been forced to give up the practice or had decided to stop doing whatever he had been doing. I thought the latter more likely since if he'd been forced to stop he surely would have found a way to warn those waiting in France that the deal was off. The caller said 'we' would give him until Friday. Several people were involved, then, and the deadline was in four days. It seemed to me important that I should meet Vernon Slater before then.

The factor which I didn't appreciate, though it was soon brought to my attention, was the alarm caused to the caller when he realised he could have betrayed enough information to make me a threat. Though he himself might be in France there must be others willing to act on his behalf right there in London. And two of them made an appearance the very next day.

It was not I who released the catch on the front door to admit them but they probably told whoever they did buzz they were tenants who'd forgotten their key. And though they did not expect to find me in, they knocked politely enough on the door of the flat.

The taller of the two young men smiled. 'Settling in all right?'

'Yes, thank you.'

'Just checking that everything's in order. If you don't mind.'

His rather bored and condescending tone of voice indicated he was a manager of the property. I opened the door wider and they walked in. And, indeed, they both showed keen interest in the condition of the flat and its furnishings.

The shorter one asked me, 'What's your line of work, sir?'

'I'm a playwright.'

'Really? That must be very interesting.'

'From time to time,' I said. Most people who don't work in the theatre seem to think it's a lighthearted *game*.

The senior man, under guise of examining the unblemished finish of the desk, was giving close attention to the scripts and papers I'd piled there. And now he had my name. 'Do you plan to stay in London for long, Mr Murray?'

'For several months, at least.'

He nodded. 'Mr Slater seems to have left everything in first-rate condition.'

'How long did he live here?' I asked.

And they did not know. They exchanged glances as though one could jog the other's memory. But the pause went on too long. They did not know. Worse, they didn't know if they *should* know. And, none too soon, I began to suspect they were not managers. The taller one tried to cover the gap. 'It must have been quite a long time. I can't remember exactly when he actually…'

I pressed the advantage. 'You *knew* Mr Slater, of course.'

'Oh, yes. Of course. Did you know him?'

I was aware that both of them awaited my answer to that with great interest. But now I had connected them with the strange telephone call and tried to set up the present dialogue several speeches ahead. 'No. I met him just once.' I smiled at the recollection. 'He seemed to be a very secretive person.'

'When was that?' the shorter man asked.

'Pardon?' His question was a bit more direct than I'd anticipated but now neither of them was concerned to keep up the pose.

'Did you meet him here?'

'Yes. He called in yesterday ... looking for something he'd forgotten to take with him. He wouldn't say what it was but he searched around a good deal.' I let them digest that in the hope they'd conclude that it was indeed Slater who'd answered the phone, whatever the man in France might have thought at the time. Naturally, Slater would be guarded with a stranger in the room listening. There was the possibility that they'd made a mistake. It would have been more helpful if the situation had allowed them to ask me directly about that call but even without a plain statement I felt I'd been able to lessen the pressure. And it seemed they thought so too for, shortly thereafter, they left.

But they did not leave the building. In fact they waited until I went out to go buy a take-away lunch before forcing the door of the flat and comprehensively searching the premises. When I got back, the door frame was splintered and everything was turned upside down. In the bedroom the bed was tipped over on its side and the contents of the wardrobe were spread over the floor. In the kitchen, the storage cabinets had been emptied and even the para-phernalia under the sink had been rooted out. All the other cupboards had been emptied. They'd even torn open the cardboard cartons I hadn't unpacked and emptied the contents all over the living room. The whole place was strewn with paper.

The intruders had been very thorough and – though I did not realise it at the time – discriminating. None of the small drawers in the desk or the sideboard had been touched. That should have told me something about the *size* of what they were searching for but, as I say, the point didn't occur to me at the time. I cleared a space to eat at and gave a lot of thought to how I should now proceed.

There was no point in calling the police. Nothing had

been stolen. And in any case it was my own fault. Perhaps if I had not invented the story that Slater came back to look for something my visitors would not have felt obliged to look for it themselves. The striking fact was, they evidently knew what they were looking for. And now I wanted to know what it could be. I also thought it imperative that I should meet Vernon Slater as soon as it could be managed.

I had not, as yet, received any mail at the flat but I knew the procedure. When the postman buzzed the porter, the main door was opened and he laid the entire package on the hall table to be sorted and delivered to the individual flats, usually by the porter's wife. There was little likelihood of Slater's mail being inadvertently delivered to me. That would be redirected to the forwarding address he'd left. But I was sure the redirected mail would be collected by the postman the following morning. If I got down before the postman I would be able to see what Slater's new address was. Of course, that assumed there would be at least one letter waiting to be forwarded. Unwilling to count on that, I sent a letter to him at Lower Sloane Street.

But my precaution was unnecessary. Early next morning I went down to examine what was set out on the hall table. Among about a dozen letters of various tenants who'd moved on there were three for Slater. I slipped them in my pocket and got back to my flat before the postman arrived. The address was 89 St Nicholas Lane, Lewes, Sussex. The letters themselves were of little interest to me and I made no attempt to find out what the envelopes contained. On all of them the original address was typewritten.

Lewes is the ancient county town of Sussex and is proud of its reputation for being rabidly anti-Catholic. They still burn the Pope in effigy every year under the guise of traditional, harmless fun. I'd missed the occasion, but it was well-attended and still a popular topic of conversation when I booked in at the White Hart Hotel. It was

66

important to do that first in case Slater wanted to check up on me. And I booked until Saturday so that I could keep a check on him. I also took the opportunity to let the reception clerk know that I was a 'mining engineer'. Since I was in time for lunch the clerk suggested I go right through to the dining room. I told him I wouldn't think of such a thing and, moreover, I wanted all my meals served in my own room.

With that sorted out I felt free to call upon Vernon Slater. I walked back along High Street towards School Hill and found St Nicholas Lane without difficulty. The house was one of a recently refurbished terrace whose effect was ruined by individually designed doors. I beat the ornate knocker. The door was opened by a tall, rather gaunt looking man.

I smiled. 'Mr Slater?'

He came nowhere near smiling. 'Yes?'

If I hoped to arouse his interest or concern it was necessary to avoid stating my ostensible purpose right away, so I began chattily enough, 'My name's Murray. I've just moved into the flat you left in London.'

He nodded, maintaining a steady disinterested look, and waited for me to go on.

I went on, 'It seemed to me the phone calls might be important so I thought I would...'

'Phone calls?' His expression didn't change but there was no hiding the anxiety in his voice.

'Yes. And since I had business here anyway...'

'Come in, Mr...?'

'Murray.'

'Mr Murray. Please come in.'

He showed me into a small but very pleasant living room and I was happy to note that his tidiness carried over from being a tenant to a householder. I sat down and he immediately wanted to know, 'How did you find me?'

I made a vague, 'silly me' gesture and tapped my pocket before taking out the three envelopes. 'As I was leaving this morning I happened to notice these had been laid out for collection. Naturally, since I was on my way to Lewes, I thought I'd cut the postal delay and deliver them myself.'

'I see,' he said. 'And you could have.'

67

There was a warning tone in that last remark but I disregarded it. 'Yes. I am. That's what I'm here for.'

'But I have a letter-box, Mr Murray. You could have slipped them into my letter-box in passing.'

I pretended some bewilderment at this and pressed on with the other point as though I hadn't understood him. 'So I thought if you were willing to give me your phone number I could pass that on … if there are any more calls.'

Again his full attention was captured and he sat down in the chair opposite me. 'What sort of calls?'

'Very strange calls, really,' I said, and began to feel like a character in an early Priestley play where the words are played like chords with a common dominant. So far the dominant note was 'calls'. He should now pick up the word 'strange'. But he didn't. Unaware of the Priestley pattern, he just waited for me to continue. He had neatly trimmed, well-brushed grey hair, dark eyes magnified by strong spectacles and a long thin neck partly disguised by a deep collar and windsor-knotted tie. He also wore a cardigan which did not disguise his thin, narrow shoulders. And he was waiting for me to tell him about the strange phone calls. I decided some ornamentation wouldn't come amiss. 'I've only been there a few days and there have been several. At first they just hung up as soon as I answered.'

'Perhaps they were wrong numbers,' he reasonably suggested.

'Yes. That's what I thought. At first. But once or twice they started telling me something and then, when I asked who was calling, they hung up.'

That pierced Slater's well-assumed complacency. I saw the chords on the side of his neck tighten and his eyes focussed even more acutely. 'What did they say?' He cleared his throat. 'I mean, did you gather what is was they started to tell you?'

I tried a confused little chuckle and made a visible effort to recall. 'It was something about … deliveries, I think. Deliveries to France.'

There was a pause, then, 'I see,' Slater said. And I could see at once I'd gone too far. He suddenly knew I was not the person I wanted him to believe in. Or knew, at least, that my purpose in visiting him was not as I'd given out. 'What is your business, Mr Murray?'

'I'm a mining engineer,' I said, and brought myself to add, 'for my sins. What do you do?'

He smiled. 'Didn't Mrs Dobbie tell you?'

'No.' I smiled right back. 'Mrs Dobbie is very discreet. She wouldn't even tell me your name.'

'But that didn't stop you.'

While there were still tatters of my pretence about me I got to my feet with a fine show of joviality. 'No, no. Ever eager to do a good deed,' I said. And, since we'd left Priestley for tele-land, added, 'In this naughty world.' God, I was making myself cringe at the dialogue. 'Would you like me to give the callers your new phone number?'

'I don't think you'll be troubled with any more callers for me,' he said, 'if you change your number.'

'I am having that done,' I assured him as he ushered me towards the door. 'In fact it may be done by the time I get back to London at the end of the week.' I paused on the threshold. 'Oh, that reminds me. Friday.'

'What?'

'One of the men who was calling from France said ... er ... it hadn't arrived, and they'd give you until Friday.' I gave him my friendliest grin. 'Maybe you can make sense of that.'

Slater shook his head. 'I'm afraid not. I've no idea what any of this means.' He pointedly glanced beyond me at the street. 'Are you staying in the town, Mr Murray?'

'Yes. The White Hart.'

Slater nodded approvingly. 'Very nice. Thank you for bringing the letters.'

Back at the hotel I settled myself in a corner of the bar to consider the next moves. And, on the whole, I was quite pleased with my Slater interview. In particular, it was satisfying that I'd managed to betray an ulterior purpose without giving the impression that I meant to. If Slater had been convinced that I was merely a busy-body or a do-gooder there would have been no reason for him to concern himself about me any further.

And, of course, if *he* was completely above board that would still be the case. I would hear nothing more of him. But there was no ignoring that sudden tensing of his interest when I'd embroidered the nature of the telephone calls. And there was no mistaking the anxiety in his replies or the tone in which they'd been delivered. In fact, there was no doubt at all that Vernon Slater considered me a nuisance or a threat. Depending on his reaction to that I would know the general area of his operations and, perhaps, their gravity.

Meanwhile, there was further background material to pursue. After a brisk walk down School Hill I found the public library on Albion Street. First, I consulted the voters' roll. Though aware that Slater would not be on it if he'd lived and worked so long in London, the roll gave me access to the rates assessment schedule. The terrace house in St Nicholas Lane was obviously not council property. Equally obvious, now that I'd seen inside it, was the fact the Slater had not suddenly found himself faced with the problem of settling into new accommodation. He may have had his furniture in store but that accommodation had been settled for a long time. It had the well-ordered air of a home which perfectly reflected its owner's taste. What I wanted to find out, however, was whether or not he had let it while he was in London.

Armed with all the relevant data I next called upon several estate agents to ask their help in finding me a small house which I could rent. I was very particular about my requirements and chief among them was the wish to be near the centre of the town – though not on the main road. A fairly quiet side street near the centre was what I had in mind. 'St Nicholas Lane or Station Street would be ideal.'

I told them I'd heard of one or two properties in that area which could be rented for quite long periods. Alas (estate agents say 'alas' a lot), I was too late. One of them had recently had exactly the sort of place I was looking for. I brightened. 'At the town centre?'

'Yes. St Nicholas Lane, in fact.' He paused and pursed his lips, as though recalling an unfortunate incident. 'But the owner had reclaimed it now.'

I played the dominant word again. 'Reclaimed?' It

70

struck me that the agent was not happy about something.

'Yes. Quite suddenly he took it out of our hands altogether.'

'Was there a sitting tenant?'

'Thankfully, no.'

'Perhaps the owner won't be staying there long.'

The agent shrugged over his loss of business. 'I really couldn't say. Mr Slater's a very unpredictable man. I mean, he gave us practically no notice whatever.'

'When?'

'When he told us he wanted the property taken off our list.'

'Yes, quite. But when was that?'

The agent consulted his schedule. 'At the very end of October. And the very next thing we knew carpets were being re-fitted and furniture delivered. Practically no notice at all.'

I nodded sympathetically. 'Mmm. Perhaps his work obliges him to change his plans.' I searched for an apt cliché. 'On the spur of the moment.'

'Hardly!' the agent said. 'The civil service doesn't do *any*thing on the spur of the moment.'

'But if he's in the Foreign Office ...' I hazarded.

'He's Trade and Industry!' the agent told me, not a moment too soon. That was the point I'd been aiming at when we started and, having got to it, I prepared to leave.

The agent detained me. 'Would you like us to contact you if there's any change in the situation?' he asked.

'Yes. Please do. I'm at the White Hart until Saturday and afterwards in London.' I gave him the address in London.

'We'll keep in touch, Mr Murray.'

I was a bit disappointed in Slater's department. I'd been betting on the Foreign Office. There they had plenty of information which could be sold abroad; and it was readily available by all accounts. Trade and Industry was less attractive. Still, I was well content with my afternoon's work as I walked back through the early dusk to my hotel. With little difficulty I borrowed *Whitaker's Almanack* from

71

the office and went to my room to await the arrival of dinner.

I'd been placed well back on the long side of the building and the window overlooked the grounds of Pelham House, well guarded by tall, bare trees. The shower of rain which started as soon as I got indoors now turned to a more concentrated downpour of sleet. Having screwed the radiator knob up to its full extent I switched on the lights and sat by the window to consider where my involvement with the unpredictable Mr Slater might lead. It depended upon how concerned he was about the implied threat I'd reported and what possible action could be taken by the caller if whatever was expected did not arrive on Friday.

Trade and Industry. I opened the almanack at that department to gather some idea of their range of operation. It was much wider than I'd imagined. And certainly there were many divisions which could have legitimate interest in European countries. Anyone who wanted to go in for smuggling in a big way could have unlimited opportunity at the DTI. The department was also responsible for a lot of research and development work, for which it had its own laboratories, as well as controlling companies registration and patents.

I was interrupted by a tap on the door and room service delivered the dinner I'd ordered. And it was very fortunate that I'd stipulated boiled potatoes. Without them I would not have connected two important components in the evidence I'd found at the flat.

The serving dishes were old-fashioned white porcelain. I took the large, flattish lid off the potato dish and laid it aside so that the rim would not stain the tablecloth. It was not until I'd finished the meal and stood up to have the things cleared away that I noticed the inside of the serving-dish lid. I was reminded of something by the way the overhead light struck the surface and the fact that the surface was glossy white which made the fine deposit glitter. The cause was the salty steam, of course, which had condensed and cooled on the lid. But the effect was strikingly similar to what I'd seen when shining a torch onto the white surface of the ceiling in the flat and wondering about the patch of glittering powder on *that* surface. I also recalled Barbara's remark about the windows of the flat being 'all steamed up'. Aloud I made the obvious progression: 'Cooking, boiling – *distilling*!' In the event, I was wrong about the actual process but right about the intention.

I seized the almanack again. The only laboratory of the department which was actually in London was that of the Government Chemist in Stamford Street, just over the Waterloo Bridge. There were, of course, a whole host of different offices of the department around Victoria, but in them the staff would be working with data on paper. What I was looking for was a place where the actual substances would be handled and tested. Stamford Street, I felt sure, was Slater's workplace.

And I was also convinced that he took his work home. He must have had some apparatus which was set on top of the sideboard where my couch was now placed – *that* would have been heavy enough to make the depressions in the carpet I'd noted. There it would be a convenient distance from the power point. The steam-heating or distillation of liquids would therefore give off vapour which condensed on the ceiling just where the mysterious patch of glittering dust had accumulated.

And this tied in with my earlier conjecture about his need to tamper with the meter. It was not that he couldn't afford to pay for the electricity. He couldn't afford to betray the fact that he was using so much of it with no apparent reason. Presumably the apparatus took a lot of power over long periods. But surely the equipment, if not the means of powering it, must have been noticed by the porter when he admitted the LEB man to read the meter. I made a mental note to ask Mrs Dobbie about that. Indeed, there was quite a lot I wanted to ask Mrs Dobbie about her long-stay and much-esteemed previous tenant. Unfortunately, others had the same idea, and they got to her first.

On the Wednesday morning I got a call from the estate agent. He was cautiously optimistic that he'd be able to give me good news and asked me to come and see him as soon as convenient. I suggested that if it was good news surely he could tell me on the telephone. But he insisted that I should come in person – no doubt to get me within his range of persuasion. So, after breakfast I walked through the rain along High Street and down School Hill towards the Ouse. I'd already guessed what the good news would be and the agent merely confirmed that Mr Slater had again changed his mind about the property in St Nicholas Lane. Apparently he'd asked if the firm would undertake letting and factoring as they had done before.

I asked, 'Did *he* come to tell you the good news?'

'No. He telephoned first thing this morning.'

'But he hasn't made a final decision yet?'

'Not yet,' the agent said, 'but we're very hopeful. And since you were so interested we told him there would be little difficulty in finding a suitable tenant.'

I gulped at this unforeseen complication. 'You told him about me?'

'Yes, of course.' The agent gave me a benign smile. 'Tenants are not easily found in the middle of winter.'

'But you mentioned me by name?'

The anxiety in my voice now got through to him and he bent his head sharply forward. 'Yes. There's nothing wrong, I hope.'

'Nothing that can't be put right,' I said, and rose to go. 'But I must warn you that Mr Slater may change his mind once again.'

I hurried from the office and had to hold the umbrella practically in front of my face against the wind and rain as I trudged up the steep hill which would take me back to Slater's house.

It was important that we have a candid talk. No matter how embarrassing it might be to have my subterfuge backfire on me, I didn't want anything I'd said to force him out of his house. And, however serious or even criminal his actions might have been, I could not overlook the ridiculous situation of my seeming bent on occupying every home he vacated. My main objective in the whole exercise was to find out why I was being harassed and, if possible, to stop it.

But my presence was no joke to Vernon Slater when he opened the door to me that morning. He was reluctant to let me in and I was reluctant to state my business until he

74

did. After some stonewalling I said, 'I've come to apologise.'

He drew the door wider and I walked into the living room which, even at that time of day, was immensely tidy. He invited me to sit down but before I could begin my host had a few things to get off his chest. It would have been too much to hope that while I was ferreting around he would be idle.

'The first thing is, Mr Murray, that you are *not* a mining engineer. You are a writer.'

'An unknown writer,' I said.

'The second thing is, you were not asked to deliver those letters to me by the Dobbies. They didn't know where the letters had gone.'

'That's true.'

He nodded and his voice took on a stronger edge. 'And isn't it true that *my* business is none of *your* damned business?'

'Perfectly true – as long as *your* business doesn't threaten my safety or peace of mind.'

He leaned back in his chair to assess how this might apply and if it could undermine his righteous approach. 'A few mistaken phone calls is not a great cause for concern.'

I then told him of the other events which had set me in pursuit of him. The threatening visit, the break-in, the damage and the probability I'd continue to be watched or otherwise embroiled in a matter which did not concern me. As I went on, it was obvious that his resolve to brazen it out was being weakened. When I mentioned my laudable reluctance to inform the police, the tense cords on his neck indicated not only faltering resolve but fear. I concluded my case by stating, 'So, I had to find some way of warning you of something I wasn't supposed to know.' This was not the whole truth, but near enough to encourage confidence.

He said, 'It seems I'm the one who should apologise.'

'You needn't apologise, but I'd be grateful if you'd take some action to resolve the problem.'

'I suppose you want to know what it's all about.'

'Yes. But I don't want you to tell me.'

Apparently this surprised him. 'Why not?'

'Because if you tell me you might regret it later – then I'd be a problem.'

He nodded and, very slowly, smiled. 'But there's nothing to stop you trying to find out for yourself.'

I ignored that possibility and asked, 'What do you propose to do?'

'Hide,' he said.

'That won't help me,' I pointed out. 'They'll think I know where you are.'

'But you won't know.'

'Quite.' It was irritating to find him obtuse. 'However, their method of finding *out* that I don't know could be unpleasant. For me.'

'You're a shrewd man, Mr Murray.' He looked at me intently through the glistening spectacles. 'What do you suggest?'

'I suggest you go on doing whatever it was you were doing. No doubt it was profitable. I can't understand why you stopped. Nor can they, apparently.'

There was a long silence during which he stared over my head, watching people pass by in the street. Eventually he asked, 'Would you like some coffee?'

'No, thank you. I would like gin, if you have it.'

'Certainly.' He got up and left the room.

And it was true that I wished he'd gone on spying or smuggling or whatever it was. He seemed to have led an exemplary life and yet had managed the difficult feat of making the state contribute to his welfare. That was a victory which had always eluded me. And if, as seemed likely, he'd managed to harness the Department of Trade and Industry to produce a profit, surely the novelty would not be too shattering. Such enterprise was certainly more worthy than the stale tittle-tattle which the legion of spies in the Foreign Office sold for peanuts. Idealists, I told myself, are always poor because they can never remember what happened last time.

He was gone much longer than it took to pour a drink but in fact he'd made coffee for himself and carried it in on a tray, together with a stiff measure of gin and a bottle of tonic for me. When we were both settled again he seemed determined to tell me the whole story and I didn't try to stop him.

Slater was Sussex-born and bred. He grew up in the little village of Chailey. It was there he met the only girl in his life and they married as soon as he was assured of his job in the civil service. He was assigned to one of the proliferating defence departments. That meant moving to Lewes at the beginning of the war to help organise essential services should the invasion come.

It was his wife, Nora, who set about finding a house, then carrying out the near impossible task of furnishing it in the face of all the restrictions and rationing. Slater looked around the beautifully furnished living-room. 'She never saw it like this,' he said. 'But this is how she would have wanted it.'

'Did she die during the war?' I asked.

'No. Oh, no. It wasn't the Germans who killed her.'

He went on to recall how they'd come through the war, survived the long period of austerity and, year by year, still managed to improve the house. When he was promoted to work in London he continued to live in Lewes, though often Nora and he would spend weekends in the city attending concerts and enjoying every moment of their time together.

They were very happy and, though unable to have children, lived what seemed to them a satisfying life. Each of them was contentedly involved outside the home as well. They were members of various clubs and community services. Nora, in particular, was devoted to the care of old people who lived alone.

Slater paused and bent his head. After a moment, and without looking at me he asked, 'Would you ... Would you like to see a photograph?'

I assumed it must be a photograph of Nora. 'Yes, I would.'

He stood up abruptly. 'I don't keep them in frames,' he explained, then most affectingly added, 'If you keep them in frames, they fade,'

He took a large, very securely bound, album from a

cabinet and I had the fleeting impression that he'd never shown it to anyone else. He didn't know if he should give it to me to hold or if he should hold it himself while he turned the pages.

He held it himself, standing by the side of my chair and leaning forward. I admired the pictures of Nora and those of the tall, dark-haired and handsome young man that Slater had been. Nora herself was not beautiful but she projected a kind of naïve freshness which was very appealing – and she kept it as she grew older.

Slater kept up a commentary of what was illustrated but I did not listen to the details of this occasion or that, nor did I much note the locations which had been chosen. Instead, what I insistently heard was love. There is no other sound in the range of the human voice which is so distinctive. This gaunt, rather dry man had once had the rare good fortune to be overwhelmingly in love.

As the pages moved towards the present, Slater was less eager to turn them. When the period approached the mid-1960s he decided he'd seen enough and put the book away. I prompted him with what had seemed an odd remark. 'You said the Germans didn't kill her.'

He tried to resume his composure. 'That's right,' he said. 'It was the drug company that killed her.'

In fact, he stated the drug company's name, but I may not.

When she was in her early forties Nora became increasingly afflicted with rheumatoid arthritis. The pain got worse and the deformity grew more crippling. A new drug was prescribed.

'It had passed all the safety tests!' Slater's voice declared this as though he was forcing it out over a ragged knife. 'Safe! All the tests from the Government Chemist to field assessment by the DHSS. It was the new, the *only* thing for treating arthritis. But a side-effect killed thousands of people. Within a year, it killed Nora.'

The rest of the story I could have guessed from that point, but he told me anyway. As a civil servant he knew there was no way of beating the system so that those who were guilty would be punished. The drug company, having gone through all the procedures, was in the clear.

And there were no questions asked when that particular drug was withdrawn. The drug company and the government department protected each other.

So Slater found another way to assuage his grief. He decided to take revenge. Very patiently he moved and applied and moved again to get into a position where he had access to the new wonder drugs which were going through the process of evaluation before being fed to the human guinea pigs. At first it was his intention to falsify results or to pollute the test samples offered by that one drug company. But they could always appeal and demand a new series of tests.

There was no appeal, however, against competition. Slater joined the pharmaceutical war which is constantly waged between the main laboratories. Thus he became involved in scientific espionage. He sold the British company's secrets to their European competitors. And those competitors then manufactured the latest marvel themselves – having claimed patent before the British company had even got to first base.

As a result of his actions they started losing the confidence of the market. When that happened they lost a lot of money, not only from new business but on their standard products as well. 'Everything went against them,' he declared triumphantly. 'I made the bastards pay dear for what they did to my wife. I made them lose. I made them squeal!'

Meanwhile, Slater was making considerable gains in return for the drug analyses he provided. 'And they supplied me with the equipment to do it,' he said. 'A beautiful machine. A spectro-analyser. That's what the men who searched the flat were looking for. That's what they want back by Friday.'

'But where is it?'

He got to his feet and beckoned me to follow him down into the basement.

What he showed me looked exactly like a hi-fi tape recorder even on fairly close inspection. But the vertical tape deck was bogus. It slid out to reveal a compact array of glass vessels and tubes surmounted by a vacuum chamber in which the sample could be bombarded by a variable frequency generator. Slater explained that even a very small quantity of the sample could be analysed to produce a comprehensive spectrogram printout. That was the information he then sent to France.

Remembering the deep indentations on the carpet I remarked, 'I thought it would be much heavier.'

'It is, when the distilled water vessel is connected. That has to be primed with several gallons.'

'What is the distilled water used for?'

'For cooling the system, and also to create the vacuum. The water is flash-heated into steam which escapes, expelling all the air from the chamber. Then it is suddenly cooled, creating a vacuum.'

I nodded. Everything suddenly connected: the weight, the steam, the crystalline deposit on the ceiling and the need for sustained surges of power.

Slater replaced the deceptive front cover and we went back up to the living room. What was not yet clear to me was why he had stopped operating and, having stopped, why he had not returned the machine to its owners. They must surely fear the device could be used against them.

'Yes,' Slater sighed. 'That's just it. They think I could use it in the opposite direction – selling what they hope to export here before they get the licence. On the other hand, the fact that I have it at all is dangerous to them if I'm found out.'

'I still don't understand why you stopped.'

'I was dismissed,' he said. 'I'm fifty-six now. It was either accept early retirement or get moved out to pasture in Agriculture and Fisheries. Either way, I'd be in no position to obtain drug samples. The department was willing to let me go but I was sure my masters in France would not be so understanding. So – I planned to just ... disappear.'

I felt bound to point out that he hadn't made a very good job of it.

'No. But you see, I'd no idea they had somebody else working in my department. He tipped them off that I was leaving.'

'Won't they be satisfied if they get the machine back?'

He shrugged despairingly. 'I'm afraid if I take the

machine back they won't let me go. I'm a damaging liability now. I always knew I would be, eventually. That was why I planned to disappear.'

I thought for a moment then told him, 'I'll take the machine back.'

Thus it was that I cut short my stay in Lewes and returned to London with extra luggage on Wednesday evening. It seemed very important to me that nobody else should find out where the previous tenant now lived. That house meant a great deal to him, and while it was possible for him to remain there, he should.

I'd already booked a place on the boat-train from Victoria and from there also I would cable to the address Slater had given me to say that *he* would be making the trip. First, though, I went back to the flat. The machine would fit into one of my large cardboard boxes. Then I called the embassy in Paris to leave an urgent message for the only official I knew there. He was a man who did some liaison work for the British Council – arranging tours for theatre companies and orchestras. The message that I was about to call upon him was to be delivered first thing the following morning. Everything was rushed. I took my passport and other papers with which to prove my identity beyond any doubt, then lifted the awkward box and went down to get a taxi to the station.

The solution which I'd persuaded Slater to accept was that I would return the machine to the man who wanted it. Since he'd stipulated Friday as the deadline we could assume that no further action would be taken until then. The intention was to let them think Slater himself was bringing it, but to specify only where and when he would arrive. If they showed any sign of wishing to detain me I would then play the innocent traveller doing a favour for a friend. And I would point out that I had an appointment at the British embassy. If they were wise they'd just accept delivery and that would be the end of the matter.

I arrived at Victoria in plenty of time for the boat-train, but as I was paying the driver, a car slewed round in front of the taxi. A man leapt from it and swept up the awkward cardboard box which contained the machine. I grabbed at it. Both the rear and front passenger door of the car were now wide open. The man evaded me and several other people to dump the box in the back seat. The car started to move as he ran alongside and clambered into the front seat. Then they roared away with doors slamming.

All the careful preparation had been for nothing. They'd kept watch on the flat and they'd seen me arrive with what could only be the very object they'd been searching for. Somewhat shaken, I took the underground back to Sloane Square. By the time I got there I'd come to terms with the situation. It was not so bad. I'd been saved a journey and the machine had been returned. Since the return of their property seemed to be the main point of conflict, it could well be that the trouble was over.

And, in a way, it was over completely – though I didn't know then. I called Paris again and cancelled my previous message. I also called Slater, but there was no reply. He did not expect to hear from me until some time the following day and had probably gone out to one of his music society meetings.

Next morning when Mrs Dobbie was delivering my mail she paused to examine the fresh joinery work on my splintered door frame. We discussed that and the unknown cause of the damage at some length. To her it seemed a fault of mine that anyone should wish to break in. And she wasn't very pleased either that I'd taken Slater's letters to make a personal delivery. I'd forgotten that he must have called the Dobbies after our first meeting. Mrs Dobbie was a plump, comfortable-looking woman who gave the impression that ever since she first reached maturity she'd been aware that there were no such things as opinions. People either thought as she thought or they were wrong.

She certainly resented my taking the letters. 'I'm not sure that wasn't illegal, Mr Murray.'

'I was just trying to be helpful.'

'We have very strict rules about the mail, you know. And especially about the forwarding address of a previous tenant.'

'I'm glad you do,' I assured her. 'It should be an entirely confidential matter.'

She seemed willing to accept my contrition now that

she'd made her point. 'Entirely confidential. Except for the police of course, or essential business.'

I smiled. 'It's very unlikely the police would want to find Mr Slater.'

'No, but Mr Dobbie insisted on seeing proper credentials – even when it was a man from the government.'

I felt a chill of apprehension gathering. 'A man from the government?' It occured to me that a colleague clearing up Slater's desk might have found something incriminating. 'When did the man call?' I asked.

'Yesterday afternoon.' She lowered her voice. 'It seems Mr Slater has retired very suddenly.'

I nodded. 'He told me that.'

'And of course there are papers that have to be signed. It's all forms and papers with the government.' She moved away across the landing to deliver some letters there.

I closed the door absent-mindedly and laid my letters unopened on the sideboard. It would be a fine irony indeed if, having escaped the people he was selling the secrets *to*, he were caught by the people he'd been stealing them *from*. Since Slater himself had not seemed to fear that possibility I'd assumed his method was undetectable. But even if he had been detected, surely it would be the police who'd call upon him. There would be no need for an official from the department to go down to Sussex.

It was still too early to phone him so I went back to my breakfast and instead got involved in the lyrics of the musical play I was writing for Barbara Cree. But that demanded too much concentration and I couldn't settle to it. I decided it might be better to deal with the corres- pondence and tried that for a while. All the time, though, the apprehension which had been alerted in my conversa- tion with Mrs Dobbie was growing. Something was *wrong* and I must phone Slater without any further delay.

Again, there was no reply. I waited fifteen minutes and tried again. No answer. There was nothing for it but to go there at once. Having dressed but not shaved I started out. The lift seemed agonisingly slow and when I got to the street there wasn't a taxi in sight. The tube would be better than waiting and hoping so I took the short-cut, running up Holbein Place to Sloane Square station. The rush-hour was over and there wasn't long to wait when I got to the main-line station.

For most of the journey my imagination was intent on devising feasible explanations for Slater's absence from the house when he ought to have been awaiting news of my reception in Paris. Gradually, a rather cynical possibility gained credence. It could be he had not trusted me as much as I'd thought. While I was returning the machine he could have taken the opportunity to get out of the country. If he had I wouldn't blame him. Certainly that must have been what he was planning when he told the estate agent to look for another tenant. Maybe he'd held to that plan and merely added my services to it.

In all of this I was quite mistaken, and I knew it as soon as I saw the house. The blinds were drawn on the windows. I did not knock on the door but asked a neighbour if Mr Slater had gone away. She told me Mr Slater was dead. As far as she knew a friend of his had called for him on the way to the music society the previous evening and found him unconscious. He died in hospital a couple of hours later.

Before going back to London I paid a visit to the estate agent. It seemed important to know whether or not he had decided to remain in that house he'd shared with Nora. The agent said the owner had definitely decided to stay. That was reassuring, in a way. He *had* been willing to trust me.

When I'd got over the shock and was able to think clearly again about the whole situation, the crucial piece of information seemed to be the 'government official' obtaining Slater's address from Mr Dobbie. There was absolutely nothing I could have done to prevent that. He'd shown credentials and I didn't doubt for a moment they were genuine. So the Dobbies could not be blamed for betraying their previous tenant.

Of course his visit had nothing to do with retirement papers or even the discovery of Slater's activities. For I also recalled Slater telling me there was someone else in his department being paid to keep an eye on the operation. Whoever that was, he must have been on his way down to Lewes at the same time as I was travelling back to London with the machine. And as he worked in the same department as Slater he'd be well-versed in the use, and abuse, of drugs.

It came down to a matter of timing. At the time when the official must have been arriving at St Nicholas Lane, I was being robbed of the coveted machine at Victoria. Both events happened before I was due to send the cable saying the machine was on its way. If Slater himself had taken it across the Channel I was sure he would not have come back alive.

But all this was conjecture. Now there was nothing more to be done, I tried to put the whole business out of my mind. One must be careful not to dramatise an accidental death into a murder. The doctors at the hospital who tried to revive Slater were convinced they were dealing with natural causes and concluded that their patient died of heart failure. There was no investigation, of course. The police could scarcely be involved in such an ordinary event. There were no suspicious circumstances.

The Horseman

Although I do not intend to make a *chapter* out of it, all this happened a good many years ago.

It was in 1960 – the last possible year in which I could feel young and idealistic – that I was marked for life. The mark is a two-inch long scar at the front of my left shoulder. It is visible and tangible enough, yet what it constantly reminds me is that the visible and the tangible is no safe guide to where reality begins. The doctor who treated the wound insisted on calling it a 'lesion' and was very puzzled by it. Of course he did not for an instant believe my version of how I came by the injury. Neither, it seems likely, will you.

To the doctor there was immistakable evidence that the rupture of the skin started *under* the skin. Since he was neither young nor idealistic he characterised the process as 'like a boil bursting'. An offensive simile. As an over-dramatic young man, my preference ran in favour of stigmata, at the very least. Certainly, there had been no boil; and all that came out was blood. The doctor told me; 'It'll soon heal up.' And it did. It healed a lot more quickly than my memory of the nightmare which had been the cause.

Probably I should not have gone in search of James Bentik. Any one of the others would have been less affected. But none of the others would have been as useful in the crisis to which I was ineluctably drawn. Not one of them, I think, would have been a suitable champion. Anyway, I was the one who found him and the one who'd insisted we must have him.

When I say 'we' I mean the group of us who met in a stickily hot upper room in St Martin's Lane to discuss the casting for a play I was writing. The producer, the director, the theatre manager and I had at last agreed on the particular quality the leading-man should possess, and three of us had no doubt that James Bentik was the actor who had it in abundance. The theatre manager was willing to accept my opinion, even though I'd been at school when I first saw Bentik and the manager had not seen him at all.

Indeed, Bentik had been off the stage for a good many years but his unexplained and premature retirement had not dimmed the gospel that he was the best Mercutio of *all* time – even when he was too old to play it. And the Mercutio quality was what we wanted: the dangerous, volatile, harum-scarum wildness barely held in check, which Bentik had first displayed in *Romeo and Juliet*. Later, he maintained aspects of the same quality in other roles.

The first difficulty was getting in touch with him. There was no entry in *Spotlight*, even when we consulted the foundation volume of the waist-high pile stacked in the corner of the office. We called Equity, but he'd stopped paying his dues long ago. They'd be able to find his last known address but that was all.

Our manager asked, 'Are we sure he's alive?'

'We'd have heard about it if he died,' the director said.

But even that wasn't certain. Bentik had gone to a lot of trouble to hide himself away and had no close friends we could think of who'd feel obliged to publish news of his death. All things considered – in the producer's view – our best course was just to get another actor. That would be easy enough. God knew, there were plenty of them. But the two of us who had to work with actors shook our heads. For it is an ironic fact that actors are cast not mainly for their ability to act well but for the personal impression they make – often in *spite* of their acting. Age and range and experience come into it of course but, essentially, they get the job for what they were born with. From the moment I started work on the play, the person I'd had in mind was James Bentik and, if it could possibly be managed, that was who I intended to have.

87

My colleagues thought I'd set myself an impossible task in trying to find the lost actor, but there was plenty of time. Our discussion was no more than a very early production meeting and a lot could change before the script was completed. As far as the producer and the manager were concerned we were foolish to discuss casting at all, so early in the project. I pointed out that – if nothing else – it was relevant to know who they could afford. Actors have price tags which do not always match their talent. The manager smiled warily. 'If you can find Bentik, we can afford him, believe me.'

'I'll find him.' But at the time I had no experience in such matters and brashly assumed that devices which work on the stage must work equally well in real life. Without quite formulating it, I set in motion the classical practice of 'imitative magic'. The Greeks obliged the gods to work for them by imitating the gods; so I would find Bentik by assuming his identity.

It would be pointless, of course, to apply to a missing persons bureau. They have neither the resources nor the muscle to find anyone who has a vested interest in being lost. Fortunately, however, Britain is a police state — though the constabulary is the least effective part of it. All our lives are policed by huge armies of officials dedicated to enforcing the view that we owe the state some service. The trick is to get them to work for you under the mistaken belief that they are working for our masters. There are now many more national agencies than there were in 1960, and since then I've used most of them for my own purposes. The DHSS will join the hunt if they sniff an abuse of the system, the Foreign Office will check its passport files, DVLC's huge and erratic Swansea computer can be harnessed. A simulated traffic violation is a sure way into the vast orchard of the police data banks. Even the Home Office can be got at through the NTVLRO in Bristol. There is no difficulty at all in enlisting the aid of any or all of these agencies. The simple key in each case is an appropriate lie.

But, for its range of interest and tenacity of purpose, the agency I chose was the Inland Revenue. To them I would pose as a penitent James Bentik. First, though, I posed as myself to obtain some basic information from Equity. The actors' trade union insists upon the admirable provision that on their lists no two actors shall have the same name. A new member whose name is already in use by somebody else must take a stage name. This applies even when the established member is using the new member's real name as a stage name and already has a perfectly good name of his own. Thus, Equity also knows which are stage names and which are real names. James Bentik, I discovered, was his real name and they'd last heard from him eight years before at an address in Hammersmith. It was then he'd told them he was leaving London.

Next, I phoned our profession's weekly newspaper, *The Stage*, and collected what information was available. That led to a contact with the director who'd last worked with Bentik. It was a production of *Romeo and Juliet* in which the actor hoped to re-establish himself at the age of forty-five by straining after the youthful Mercutio once again. 'It was a bloody awful experience,' the director told me, 'even without the Tybalt business. But after *that*, of course, he just couldn't go on.' When I asked what 'the Tybalt business' was, there came a noticable silence at the other end of the line. And my eager prompting did little to clarify the matter. The director ended our conversation. 'If you don't know about it, I'd rather not say. I'd hate to do him more harm than he's already done himself.'

Shortly thereafter, the tax office at Ebury House in Victoria Street received a telephone call from a James Bentik – an actor who'd just returned from abroad with a view to working again in London. He'd been told to get in touch with the Pimlico branch by Provincial 3 in Bradford. He seemed very evasive about where he'd been since he left Hammersmith. The clerk took note of that address. Bentik asked for an immediate appointment. Of course that wouldn't do. The officers in Victoria Street wouldn't *think* of talking to anyone until they had a decent pile of comprehensively stapled paper to mull over. The man insisted that he had not worked in Britain for eight years but refused to be specific about exactly where he *had* worked. He grew quite stroppy and only after pressing would he say where he was living at that moment. He

89

gave the address of the friend who was giving him shelter – a playwright called Howard Murray.

Having set that gear in train, my full attention returned to writing the play. After a few days the tax office had another, now angry, call from Bentik asking to speak to the officer in charge of his file. The officer declined to speak but the clerk said they'd be writing to him very soon. Three weeks later – which is very soon indeed for Ebury House – a well-filled buff envelope addressed to Bentik was delivered to my flat. By that time my preoccupation with the actor had so influenced the play, and the leading character, it was impossible for me to see anyone else in the part. And all the other characters were affected by that perception. The intricate mechanism which enables a play to work now had its mainspring coiled around James Bentik.

The envelope from the tax office contained the standard tax return form, a few leaflets and a letter. The letter was severe in tone, under the guise of merely establishing some facts which seemed to be in dispute. Mr Bentik was asked to confirm that when he left Hammersmith he did *not* go abroad. Was it not true that, initially at least, he'd gone to Scotland? Was he not employed there by the Pitlochry Festival Theatre in the summer of 1951? And had he not received this letter (copy enclosed) dated 3 June 1952 from our Inspector in Perth? Apparently things looked pretty bleak for Mr Bentik if he hoped to get off scot-free. Not only was the Inspector in Perth still awaiting a reply; he also hoped for early settlement of the sum due, which the Collector of Taxes would be glad to receive.

I smiled at this additional production cost. For it seemed to me only fair that if I betrayed Bentik to the Inland Revenue then the management should pay the debt. But that would be met some time in the future. Meanwhile, it was clear that if the tax men lost track of him in Perthshire that was where I must go. I'd had some dealings with the theatre at Pitlochry and I knew the staff there to be impeccable record-keepers. Before I set out, though, it was an easy matter to check on the programme for the '51 season. To my dismay, the cast list of that year's company did *not* include James Bentik. Nor was he listed in subsequent years. Why, I wondered, would a management pay an actor who did not appear? There were other names I recognised: Edward Jewesbury, Joss Ackland, Graham Crowden and a young John Fraser. The big production of the season was *Macbeth* for which all hands would have had to be on deck. Yet there was no mention of James Bentik.

It was at this point in the affair that a strange kind of *un*reason began to dominate my actions. Obviously, there was no point in applying to the Pitlochry Theatre if they had not employed the man I was searching for. There was a slight chance that he'd been engaged to play and had been paid for rehearsals before he left the company or was sacked. But in those circumstances he certainly would not have remained deep in the fastness of the Scottish highlands. And that was almost ten years ago. All these factors argued against my taking the journey north; yet something lured me on. No. That isn't true, either. I'm just trying to offer a justification in retrospect for something which required no justification at the time. It was necessary to follow wherever the trail led and there might be some *irr*ational explanation which I could depend on and follow through.

I took a sleeper on the overnight train to Perth. It was on one of the last great steam monsters of the line. As I walked up the platform, through gritty clouds of vapour which occasionally obscured the greenish lamps of Euston, my mind kept restating a warning about 'the fiend that lies like truth'. This caused a feeling of apprehension, but I could not place the words in context until that fruitful moment which occurs just before one falls asleep. It was from *Macbeth*, of course. The fiend that lies like truth assures Macbeth that he'll be perfectly all right – 'till Birnam wood do come to Dunsinane'. The bloody-handed Thane accepts the assurance as a seal of invulnerability because he cannot imagine trees walking across a wide valley and climbing a steep hill. But when his enemies come for him they advance on Dunsinane camouflaged with branches they have stripped from Birnam Wood. Both of these places are just down the road from Pitlochry Theatre and, as I now recalled, in their production of

Macbeth the actors were camouflaged in real Birnam foliage. Again, imitative magic. As I dozed off, that seemed to me important.

However, there is little which is magical about Perth station far too early in the morning. One has the impression that whoever built it spent so much money on the large and imposing shell they couldn't afford to furnish it. A taxi took me to the Salutation Hotel where I went to bed again to bridge the gap between dawn and sunrise. After breakfast I hired a car and drove a further thirty miles north to the Festival Theatre. On the way – apart from being seduced once more by the lush beauty of Tayside – my thoughts kept coming back to that sudden silence on the telephone when I was talking to the last director who'd worked with the missing actor. He didn't want to do any more harm than Bentik had done himself. What was it the actor had done which even the gossips of the theatre didn't want to talk about? Considering the outrageous stories they freely bandied about, it was difficult to imagine *any* just cause for reticence.

At the box office I gave my name and asked to see Kenneth Ireland. He ran the place. In fact, without him the Festival Theatre would not have survived and certainly would not have flourished. It has fallen on hard times and crass judgement now, but right up until 1983 the man whose spirit dominated Pitlochry was Kenneth Ireland. From earlier dealings I knew he had almost total recall of the people who'd worked for him. I asked, 'What happened with James Bentik in the '51 season?'

'Bentik.' Kenneth pursed his neatly moustached upper lip reflectively. 'James Bentik. He was a great Mercutio, wasn't he?'

'Yes, that's the one.'

'We've never done *Romeo and Juliet*. In my opinion, the play just falls apart after the banishment.'

'Kenneth, I couldn't agree more; but did you employ Bentik for other roles?'

The wary eyes behind the glistening spectacles did not blink. 'I don't think he has ever acted here.'

There was something about the careful choice of the theatre man's words which alerted me. Kenneth Ireland, I knew, had served in the Intelligence Corps during the war. It seemed worth insisting. 'That is not what I asked.'

He smiled, paused, then, 'Strictly speaking,' he conceded.

'So? Strictly speaking – did you employ him, whether or not he appeared?'

'You seem to be sure that we did.'

'*I* am not sure. The Inland Revenue is sure.'

'Is that who wants to find him?'

'No. I'm the one who wants to find him. What happened? Why didn't he appear?'

Kenneth got up to replenish the small dish of potato crisps which I'd been wolfing with my drink. We were seated in the drawing room of the large Scottish baronial house which overlooked the theatre. Odd, I thought, that a man renowned for his autocratic directness of speech should be so evasive. And now, even if I'd not been looking for Bentik to fill a tailor-made part, I would have been determined to find him just to clear up the mystery. My dutiful host also replenished my glass before he returned to the chair opposite me. He placed his fingertips together and regarded me carefully over the bridge they made. 'James Bentik was not well. He became ill shortly after he arrived to start rehearsals.'

'Ah! So he went back to London?'

'No, he was taken to Perth Infirmary.'

That seemed fairly straightforward. The actor was hired for the season, became ill, went to hospital and continued to be paid while it was thought he might recover soon enough to rejoin the company. What was *not* straightforward was Kenneth's attempted evasion of these simple facts. 'Then why all the mystery?'

'It's not a mystery to me,' he said. 'More … a secret.'

I smiled. The distinction was nice. And for several moments I considered whether or not I'd be wise in trying to overcome the polite but firm barrier which had been placed in my path. Nowadays, I shy away from other people's secrets because I have too many of my own. But I was young and brash then; and convinced of my right to know everything. 'I'm not going to give up so easily.' I said. 'Surely it's not a secret that he was ill and went to hospital.'

'No. I expect you could have found that out from other people.'

'So, the secret must be why he retired and where he is now. And since you are being so cagey you must know the answer to both questions. Do you?'

'Yes.'

I tried a reasonable argument. 'If you help me, you'll be helping him. There is a marvellous part I'm writing for him. It would be a shame to deprive him of that opportunity.'

Kenneth gave me an expressionless stare which still managed to convey the fact that he saw through my ploy and was well able to judge how much of my interest was playwright bountiful and how much vulgar hunter. He took a studied sip of his own drink before he said, 'I hope it's a modern play.' Then, a faint smile, 'Nothing with swords.'

'No, no,' I laughed. 'He's too old to play Mercutio now.' But there was something odd in the warning and the tone of voice in which it had been delivered. This prompted me to ask, 'Why should he not use a sword? He had the reputation as a good swordsman.'

'Far too good,' Kenneth said, then gradually unfolded the whole chilling story of how Bentik had been forced to retire.

I'm tempted to report exactly what he said without explanation but probably that would be too high-handed for those who don't see *Romeo and Juliet* at least twice a year. Some idea of the characters and how they are involved is essential if one is to understand the enormity of Bentik's crime and the danger in which, later, I found myself.

Even if you've never seen the play you probably know that the strife is between two prominent families: the Montagues and the Capulets. The doubt over which is which would be solved if the principals were given their full names. We should speak of Romeo Montague and Juliet Capulet. They fall in love while the rest of their respective families and kinsmen remain at daggers drawn. There are brawls in the streets and Escalus, the Prince of Verona, does not take it at all well. He warns those who may be found guilty of any further trouble, 'Your lives shall pay the forfeit of the peace.' But there *is* more trouble, and when Tybalt is slain the Prince pronounces banishment on his killer and appoints avenging soldiers to carry out immediate retribution if the culprit is found within his domain.

The most spirited of the Montague supporters is Mercutio, while the champion of the Capulets is Tybalt. The whole tragedy is set in train when, during a confused swordfight, Tybalt kills Mercutio. That is the act of violence which sets everything else in motion – Tybalt kills Mercutio. Of course Tybalt is meant to be the superior swordsman. In the play's unalterable plot it is not surprising that Tybalt, the famed dueller, kills the erratic dreamer Mercutio. However, the last time Bentik played Mercutio it was *he* who emerged from the duel. On that dreadful night, Mercutio killed *Tybalt*. The actor playing Tybalt was a young man called Sean Carrick and by the end of Act III scene i, Sean Carrick was dead.

The performance took place in Bucharest. It was part of a cultural tour sponsored by the British Council. The Romanian officials who were called to the theatre did all they could to suppress the true facts of the case and to give other reasons why the English company's visit was being cut short. They were abetted by the company who, one to the other, convinced themselves that Sean Carrick had accidently fallen on his own sword.

And that was what they told the young man's family when they brought the body home. But James Bentik took no part in this well-meant conspiracy. He was totally shattered by what he had done. And, of course, the other actors on the stage at the time saw clearly what happened. They were sworn to secrecy by the director. 'So,' Kenneth concluded, 'it became one of those unspoken facts which people know is there only by the shadow it casts.'

'What happened at the *Macbeth* rehearsals here?'

He sighed. 'Bentik was cast as Macduff.'

That meant another swordfight, though at the end of the play. It is Macduff who kills Macbeth. And, before that, Macduff is one of those who storms Dunsinane under cover of the foliage from Birnam Wood. This seemed to me a potent mixture which must result in disaster. I asked, 'Did you know about what had happened in Bucharest when you hired Bentik?'

'No! Certainly not. But there was another member of our company that year who'd been onstage in Bucharest when Sean Carrick was killed.'

Everything, it seemed, had conspired against the once and greatest Mercutio. I could see exactly how fraught the situation must have been for him. In his effort to escape from the past he banished himself into the remote hills of Scotland only to find there the danger of repetition and an accusing face. I stated, 'He didn't go into hospital, did he?'

'No,' Kenneth said. 'He went into hiding. He took a little cottage on the edge of Rannoch Moor. That was ten years ago – and he's still there.'

As I drove back to the hotel in Perth it was my intention to forget all about casting Bentik in my own play. If, as Kenneth believed, the actor suffered a kind of nervous breakdown, and still felt himself hunted, it was unlikely he could be drawn back to the stage. And probably it would be unwise to have him, even if he were willing. But the story I'd just been told could not be put out of my mind. For one man to kill another in the course of entertainment was bad enough, but it was not that fact which fascinated me. With youthful callousness, my imagination dwelt on the hubris, not the murder or the victim.

Mercutio fought Tybalt – and *won*! That went against all the laws of drama. There is no conflict without cause. And if it is *Mercutio* who kills Tybalt then Romeo will not be banished for the crime. And if he is not banished then neither of the young lovers need die. The whole inexorable train of misunderstandings is derailed and the play is brought up short with nowhere to go. But the tragedy averted in Verona may well have taken its toll on Rannoch Moor.

It was in that frame of mind that I made a slight detour near Dunkeld and stopped the car at Birnam Wood. In 1960 it was not an imposing sight – and it is even less imposing now. But the trees had once stretched much further south and east along the banks of the Tay. On the other side of the river the stone of destiny was housed at Scone and above it was the hill fort of Dunsinane. On that warm summer afternoon I shivered – not because I found myself in the presence of history but more, I think, because I found myself in the presence of art; which still is much more real to me. The shivering, slightly fearful, sensation made me decide that I must go to meet James Bentik after all. There was also an obligation of courtesy. I'd been told the actor's secret only because I was willing to offer him work.

I checked out of the Salutation Hotel – not much changed since the Young Pretender plotted victory there – and headed beyond Pitlochry on the B846 by the side of Loch Tummel and Loch Rannoch. There was a charming simplicity about the directions I'd been given. I was to keep going until I ran out of road. Eventually, that was accomplished. Transport thereafter was on foot or pony. There were pony-trekking stables offering reasonable rates but I decided to walk – about three miles, I'd been told. The actor had certainly taken his self-imposed banishment seriously. His cottage would be the second one I encountered and would be seen about a half-mile north of the track through a gap in the hills.

That walk through the desolate beauty of the highlands in bright sunlight is now burned on my memory, though at the time it was burned on my feet. The leather soles of my city shoes soon became polished by the coarse grass and it became impossible to ascend even the gentlest rise without slipping and falling. To avoid this, I sought the rougher ground and so added heel blisters to my general discomfort. But at last I did see the small, stone-built cottage in the distance. There was no sign at all that it was inhabited. But then, in the three miles I'd walked, there was no sign that *Scotland* was inhabited.

When I knocked on the door I was kept waiting for a long time before it was opened by a man with the most vivid blue eyes I have ever seen. He was a short, grey-haired, middle-aged man, but none of that was apparent for several moments. All I could see were his eyes caught in the sunlight, framed in the shadow of the doorway. He asked, 'What do you want?'

'I'm looking for James Bentik,' I said.

'Yes? I'm James Bentik.'

It was difficult to believe him. The man I'd been searching for, that I'd carried around in my mind, that had caught and held my imagination for so long, was taller, younger, more commanding. This man would never be able to fill the role I'd written for him – though his eyes might pierce it through. Nevertheless, I told him, 'My name is Howard Murray. I'm a playwright.' To this, quite shamelessly, I added a lie. 'Kenneth Ireland suggested I should come to see you.'

'What about?'

His question found me wretchedly ill-prepared. I'd cast myself in a scene which had to go on although the plot had changed. Until a more suitable ad lib occurred to me it was obviously better to try for an entrance than face a baffled exit across a three-mile stage. 'May I come in?'

He stepped back out of the sunlight and opened the door wider for me to follow him. Once over the threshold we were already in the main room of the cottage. It was both living room and kitchen. He was saying, 'I haven't seen Kenneth for a long time. How is he?'

'Very well.' But all the time my brain was racing to come up with a completely new project which might fit the sparse facts at my disposal. I was a playwright. A theatre director had suggested that I get advice from an actor. The actor was a famous Mercutio. The only thing which might connect these ingredients prompted another, bolder, lie. 'Kenneth suggested that you'd be the best person to help me with a play I'm writing. It's a modern reworking of *Romeo and Juliet*.' The boldness of this ploy lay in the fact I would not have said such a thing if I knew the truth about the performance in Bucharest.

He stopped and turned so suddenly in the middle of the room that I almost walked into him. His eyes searched my face, 'You!' It had been an involuntary exclamation and he went on as though forcing himself to sound natural. 'You might be just the person I've been waiting for.'

'Were you waiting for someone?'

'Oh, yes!' His eyes probed into mine as though wondering if he could trust me. 'And lately I was sure you were coming, though I didn't know who you would be.'

If I'd been wise my next move would have been to walk right out again and head for the hills, but I was held by the oddness of his statement and a foolish belief in my own ability to cope with eccentric behaviour. So – 'Really?' I gave a little laugh. 'Then perhaps I'll be able to help *you*.'

'I hope so,' Bentik said fervently. 'I do hope so.'

After that revealing moment he reclaimed his social graces from too long ago – invited me to sit down, offered me a drink and generally presented a cameo performance of the willing host. During this, I gave some attention to the room and its decorations. One end of it was quite comfortably furnished and there were a lot of photographs and mementos of the stage. The most striking of these was Hirschfeld's famous caricature of Bentik as Mercutio. Evidently, this was the original drawing which had been done for the *New Yorker*; to which the artist had added a personal dedication. There were reminders of many roles he'd played with great success. In Shakespeare: Ariel, Laertes (for which he probably learned to fence), Hotspur and Lear's antic but sad Fool. In modern plays: the psychopathic Danny in a revival of *Night Must Fall*, and Tom in *Outward Bound*. What they had in common, I suppose, was erratic nervous energy. But one always came back to his most celebrated role. And there, on the wall above the hearth, was Mercutio's sword. Bentik turned and caught me staring at it.

He remarked, 'Yes. I always used that sword. Much better to have the real thing than trust those props costume designers always want.'

I was finding it difficult to remember he didn't know that I knew. Even so, it must have occurred to him that if he'd used a prop sword he could not have killed a man and would have saved himself and others a lot of grief. He handed me a large glass of cider and drank his own from a pewter mug. I jolted into my performance and, rather like

99

a legionnaire coming upon an unexpected oasis, grabbed at the drink. 'Excellent!' I told him. 'This is *just* what I need.' I'd never drunk cider before in my life but it was probably all Bentik had in the refreshment line.

He sat down opposite me in an ancient armchair and I braced myself for instant invention on my purpose and how Bentik could help me with it. But I was spared the effort. Instead, the conversation plunged directly into what use I could be to *him*. He began by asking me to stay with him in the cottage 'for a few days' and before I could find any excuses went on to insist that it was an emergency precaution. His health had been failing again and he feared that a crisis might occur when he had no means of calling help.

'What does your doctor suggest?' I asked, implying that if he was ill he'd no right to exploit it in the middle of nowhere. 'Perhaps you need hospital treatment.'

He uttered a grunt and waved a bony hand. 'Doctors! Hospitals! They are no use to me. But you could be.' He leaned forward and once again his eyes made everything else blur into the background. 'What I need is someone who can fight demons.'

I was startled. 'And you think *I* can?'

He slumped back again. 'I don't know. I don't know if you can or not. But at least you know who they are.' He closed his eyes wearily. 'And I know *why* they are.'

To anyone outside the theatre this sort of heightened imagery will seem fanciful. But actors are used to feeding on their own imagination and I'd been told stranger things by others in the profession – albeit when they were drunk. Bentik was not drunk. But on those occasions, and on this, I did not for a moment doubt the sanity of my informants. In artists of all sorts, the subconscious is not buried under layers of unproductive matter. It is tilted up on edge and often breaks the surface. This is a necessity to allow for easy access by individuals who often have to refer to it in order to earn a living. Mine was in that position from an early age. Clearly, whatever demons pursued Bentik arose from the situation and the play which I'd claimed to be reworking. In the silence I began to rehearse *Romeo and Juliet* in my mind. The process was interrupted.

'I'm an epileptic,' the man said quietly. 'And I feel the charge building up again.'

'In that case,' I told him, 'I'll stay.'

He seemed surprised by so positive a response. 'Most people are afraid of it.'

'Only because it's something they don't understand.'

'But you do?' He nodded as though this merely confirmed his hopes of me. 'You understand that – as *well*.'

'I had an uncle who often stayed with us when I was a boy. He was epileptic and I was young enough to get used to it,' I told him.

And, indeed, I did fully realise the injustice which ignorance attaches to epilepsy. There was absolutely no point in his being in hospital. Lying in bed and being watched by strangers would not prevent a seizure.

But there was something else for me to note about this new fact. It fitted perfectly with my vague feeling that I had not arrived where I was needed entirely of my own volition. At first it may have seemed to me that I was deciding what to do and where to go. That was no longer credible. Before I'd left London the records available to me indicated there was no point in travelling to Scotland – yet I came. And then, when Kenneth Ireland had warned me of Bentik's condition, it was clear he'd be of little use in the object I'd started with – yet I continued. Finally, when I actually saw Bentik, there was no question of his having any part in my immediate plans – yet I remained. It seemed relevant to conclude that one should resort to imitative magic only with great care; for when you make use of it – it also makes use of *you*. While the sun was still up I went back to the car for my bag. When approaching the cottage again it struck me that the third hike over those three miles seemed much less tiring than the first.

The cottage had once been a wayside inn on the old and fabled 'road to the Isles' and it was built to last. The rough stones which made up its thick walls were the stones of the moor, gouged out of the Grampians at the end of the Ice Age and scattered as soon as the sun was strong enough to make rivers out of glaciers. The dwelling made of this ancient granite had been converted and improved – but not very much. Living arrangements were still basic. Water had to be collected from a spring outside. And outside, also, was the soil lavatory. Heating and cooking facilities were joined in the cast-iron kitchen range which occupied what had been a wide hearth. The fuel was peat or wood. Lighting was by oil lamps. There were only two rooms. I was to sleep on a couch in the living room/kitchen while Bentik slept in the bedroom. He seemed remarkably well adapted to this bare existence and at first was impatient with my willingness to help with the chores. But I insisted. It passed the time.

The following day when I drove into Kinloch Rannoch for supplies, the distance from the road-end to the cottage seemed little more than a pleasant stroll in the rope sandals Bentik lent me. On the way I considered how epilepsy, even in its milder form, might have been to blame for the tragedy in Bucharest. I also decided that if I were going to be any help I'd have to admit knowing about that, or get him to tell me about it.

First I tried getting him to tell me. But I was no good at the oblique, time-wasting technique needed to coax it out of him. If he thought nothing of making demands on my time then the least he could expect me to demand of him was honesty. On the second night, when the curtains were drawn and we were settled on either side of the fire reading, I asked, 'Mr Bentik, why did you retire from the stage?'

While still keeping his head in position to read the book on his knee, he raised his eyes so that he stared at me from under his brows. 'I think you know,' he said, and went on reading.

Since he was right there was no alternative for me but to do the same. After a long pause in which the only sound was the turning of pages, it seemed worthwhile remarking, 'I'm sure it was an accident.'

'No,' Bentik said. 'At the moment when it was happening, I wanted to kill Tybalt.' He closed the book and straightened in his chair. 'If it had been an accident there would be no need for me to feel guilty.' I was about to interrupt but he raised a hand to forestall it. 'And an accident would have been forgiven.'

'By whom?'

'By the Prince. He would not have sent his horseman searching for me all these years.'

The moment he said that the whole picture was presented to me complete. The consequences of the stage duel could not be avoided because they too were in the play. As far as Bentik was concerned the curtain was still up on that performance because his own action had ensured that it could not end. Since he, not Romeo, killed Tybalt the action could not advance beyond that point. There were no lines or scenes to cover it. So the sentence passed by the Prince of Verona still hung over him. And would be enforced, apparently, by one of the Prince's mounted soldiers armed with a lance. The lamplight in that old, still room was not strong enough to illuminate the corners and the tallowy smell of the flame did a lot to heighten the sudden alarm I felt at being isolated with a man who believed these things to be true. As evenly as I could manage, I asked him, 'When did you first become affected by epilepsy?'

'About ten years ago.'

'That's when you came to rehearse *Macbeth*.'

He nodded. 'And that's when I heard the hoofbeats. Far in the distance then, but getting closer.' He gave me a charming, self-deprecating smile as though well aware that the truth as he knew it was not acceptable by others. He added, 'When it comes, it seems to come in summer. But maybe that's only because the snow in winter muffles the sound.'

It will be as obvious to you as it was to me that what Bentik suffered from and feared was a disease and not a vengeful horseman. In partial seizure, auditory and other hallucinations are common – as is temporary paralysis. Obviously, his sense of guilt interpreted the effects of the disease in terms of what had caused the guilt. All these things were perfectly clear to me at that moment. But – at that moment, I did not have the scar on my left shoulder.

As Bentik had warned me, the 'charge' was gathering power in him. During the next couple of days I noticed the signs. His fingers began to tremble; slightly at first, then markedly and for longer periods. His astonishing eyes dimmed. His upright fencer's posture slackened and his speech became curiously furry. But most unnerving by far – he was listening all the time. Often I had to repeat remarks several times in order to get through to his attention, which was concentrated on the moorland outside. He gave me sharp looks of annoyance and gradually we stopped talking. That is, *I* stopped talking. Unnoticed by me, he'd already stopped some time earlier.

As the week went on he spent most of the day in the bedroom – waiting. He was reluctant to eat and grew weaker. He stopped shaving and the grey stubble on his face made his healthy complexion look pallid. He seemed to have difficulty keeping his eyes open. Taken altogether, I thought he was willing himself to die, and that made me angry. I accused him of it. Late in the afternoon he was lying fully-clothed on the unmade bed. Though certainly awake, he did not open his eyes at any point during my long tirade and at the end of it he spoke with great difficulty. The words came out like small furry animals escaping from a trap. 'It doesn't … *matter* now. You don't believe me.' He sighed. 'I thought … *you* would believe me.'

I slammed out of the cottage and went stamping up the hillside to a level stretch of moor. The day was overcast and, away to the east, rain clouds covered all but the lower slopes of Schiehallion. It was as though nature too was contributing to the frustrated, tense atmosphere by holding back a thunderstorm which had been promised since first light that morning.

Did I believe him? No. He was right. I didn't believe him. But I was sure *he* believed he was being hunted for a crime. It was not an accident. While it was happening, he'd told me, he wanted to kill Tybalt. And that was the crucial fact. It was the murder of Tybalt which had to be avenged – not the murder of Sean Carrick who'd been playing the part. It followed, therefore, that the person being hunted was Mercutio – not James Bentik. I could understand all that. Yes! However angrily, I could reason that out. I could also reason that it was likely he'd hear hoofbeats in the summer, since there were pony-trekking stables just a few miles away and the pony trails must occasionally pass the cottage.

My pace slackened as I walked over the expanse of short, coarse turf and the anger gave way to regret. It had been something of an affront to my pride when Bentik as much as told me I'd turned out to be a failure. He'd welcomed me eagerly – sure that I would be equal to the challenge he faced – and now found that I was chained to the same world of doctors and facts and reason which everybody else inhabited. Clearly, I was lacking in competence where it mattered most. Yet I did *want* to believe him; to believe *in* him. And that, undoubtedly, was what tipped the scales and governed what I felt compelled to do much later the same day.

When I got back to the cottage Bentik had come out of the bedroom and was sitting in his armchair by the fire. But his manner was as lost and depressed as before. It was now after six o'clock in the evening and time to prepare some food. I asked him if he wanted anything to eat and he shook his head. Nor could I convince myself that I was hungry enough to go through the long and tedious balancing act required to cook anything on the primitive range. Instead, I settled down with a book. And I still remember what the book was. Everything about that dreadful evening persists with startling clarity. The book was *Howards End* and this was my third or fourth journey through it. Before long I had to move to the window as daylight faded. I became so engrossed in the malignant goblins walking across the universe from end to end, in the 'panic and emptiness' so bravely described, that for a long time I forgot about the figure huddled in the armchair – now completely in shadow.

I moved to the fireplace in order to light the lamp which stood on the mantelshelf. But before the lamp was lit I noticed the change. As I struck the match I almost threw it away in the shock of seeing how Bentik had changed. He sat rigidly erect in the chair with his neck stretched taut. His hands were white with the tension of gripping the padded arms of the chair. His mouth was open and he seemed to be struggling for breath. With frantic fumbling I lit the lamp and looked closer. His eyes were staring wide – held balefully wide – and the colour was not vivid blue but glittering black.

I placed the lamp on the floor by his feet then loosened his belt. Next, I inserted two fingers into his mouth and uncurled his tongue. These were things I'd learned as a boy. Then, too, my uncle had asked me to take care that he was lying down in case convulsions might follow the paralysis but, since Bentik was already sitting down and unlikely to injure himself by falling, there was nothing more I could do. That is to say, nothing more I could do about the seizure. As I knelt by the side of his chair he suddenly twisted his stretched neck to look at the window. I turned in the same direction. The curtain was not yet drawn and beyond the small reflecting panes there was just blackness. He was listening. No. He was hearing something, outside. I strained to hear it and, to my horror, I *could*. We both heard the sound of hoofbeats.

It was the sound of a cantering horse. It did not pass by. It seemed to be circling the cottage at some distance. When I moved my attention in towards the room again Bentik's wide eyes were staring at me. He knew I could hear it too. He saw the fear in my face and that seemed to reassure him. His eyelids fluttered as the only acknowledgement he could muster. He knew that, though transfixed and helpless, he was not alone.

I continued to kneel beside him, staring at the rise and fall of his chest, ready to act immediately if he stopped breathing. Outside, the horseman continued his search; drawing close then receding, traversing the ridges on one side of the cottage and then the other. Sometimes, for long periods, he must have held his mount stock still while he surveyed the moor and the hills. He had only to come a little closer and he would see the cottage crouched in the hollow. I'd never felt so frightened in my life before; nor have I since – and that was more than twenty-five years ago.

When the hoofbeats were approaching I could think only: He has found us; but when the sound receded again

106

I was able to ease my cramped limbs and consider that, really, I was meant to find James Bentik and to be with him when the crisis came. All the careful trickery and deduction which enabled me to find him was no more than subterfuge by other forces which compelled me to arrive in time. Bentik had *expected* someone to help. That had been the clear implication when he first opened the door to me. I glanced at him now, held in stark immobility as though he'd been caught staring into hell and the moment had frozen.

Yes. However it had been achieved, I was there. But what was I to do? The thought came back to me of the methods I had used to find him. I'd posed as Bentik. Later, I saw myself standing in the shadow of Birnam Wood and thinking of the production at Pitlochry when Bentik had first been afflicted. What was common throughout was the use of imitative magic. Suddenly, and very loudly, the hoofbeats galloped into a closer position. The horseman could see the cottage now. I looked up at Bentik's face. The stretched tension was even greater as he reached the peak of his terror. With great effort he moved his head, twisting on the taut neck and tilted it slightly so that his uncontrolled eyes were staring at the sword.

I'd set down the lamp on the edge of the carpet and the slightly uneven surface caused the wick to smoke. It was through that coil of rising smoke I saw the soft gleam reflected from the blade above the fireplace. Though Bentik could not move his body nor speak, I knew he was urging me to take it down; to arm myself. And at the same instant the hoofbeats shuffled to a halt and the horse whinnied. The horseman was waiting. I leapt to my feet and seized the weapon, wrenching it out of the clasps which held it against the wall. With Mercutio's sword in my hand I faced the old actor again. And again there was that feverish flutter of his eyelids. *This* was what I had to do. Almost in a trance I moved to the door and drew it open, and left it open as I walked out into the dark.

The horseman seemed to have stopped somewhere ahead of me and, with the total conviction that I was being watched, I moved quickly aside to avoid being silhouetted against the lighted doorway or windows. Immediately,

107

there was the sound of the horse prancing in a tight circle as it was reined around and then the deep coughing noise of expelled breath as the bit tightened in its mouth. My eyes were becoming accustomed to the dark and I could make out the distant hills against the sky, but nearer the cottage everything seemed murky and grey. Fear may have amplified the sounds, but I was sure the horseman was just beyond the rise, at the centre of the level piece of moorland which I'd walked over earlier in the day.

I started in that direction. And, once more, my movement seemed to produce a reciprocal movement from the watching horseman. The hoofbeats drew rapidly away. That enabled me to get up onto the level ground. The crest of the rise was about a hundred yards from the cottage and when I reached that position I looked back. The door was still wide open and there was no sign of Bentik there or at the windows. The lamplight spilled out in neat elongated rectangles and where it fell across the ground the grass was turned an unreal shade of green. Now on the level ground I advanced more cautiously, trying to remember any deep ruts or potholes which might prove a hazard. In a position which gave me freedom of evasion in any direction I gripped tight on the handle of the sword and waited. I tried to think of something to shout either in defiance or as a spell. In other circumstances there would have been no difficulty in quoting many of Mercutio's lines but in that state of high tension they all deserted me. What kept recurring were lines I'd learned in school and had not ever repeated since then. It was Tom o' Bedlam's song and, more to reassure myself than frighten any adversary, I declaimed it loudly.

'With a host of furious fancies,
Whereof I am commander,
With a burning spear
And a horse of air
To the wilderness I wander;

The hoofbeats started their approach from the far end of the clearing. As they grew faster and louder I tried to drown out the sound and shouted;

'By a knight of ghosts and shadows
I summoned am to tourney...'

But now I could *see* him and the breath froze in my throat.
A huge black mass thundered upon me and, jutting from
the mass, the clearly defined shaft of a lance.

I dropped on one knee and swept my sword up to
deflect the blow above my head. There was no feeling of
impact on the sword but the earth on which I was
crouching vibrated with the weight of the animal as it
galloped past and I felt the rush of air in its wake. With
expert ease the rider wheeled about and I rose to meet
him. This time I jumped aside as he was passing and tried
to slash at the gauntlet which held the lance. Before he
could turn, I got to my feet and ran to the edge of the
clearing.

I'd realised how foolish it was to give the horseman
space to wheel and manoeuvre. In this unequal struggle
my only hope was to tempt him to the edge of the clearing
so that any charge would carry the horse over the crest of
the rise and down the hill. I glanced down into the hollow.
The cottage looked unreal with its open door and
unguarded windows streaming with light. I ran on
towards the very edge of the rise.

But the horseman turned his mount around more
quickly than I thought possible. And he guessed my
intention for he tried to head me off. Spurred into action,
the horse reared, then increased its thundering pace
towards me. I kept running to cross the path of the
advance. Faced with a moving target the rider made the
mistake of couching the lance at too wide an angle. It
struck a light, glancing blow on my shoulder but even that
upset his balance for, at the same moment, his mount
plunged downhill. The horseman was wrenched out of
the saddle. I threw myself towards the figure on the
ground and practically fell upon him with the sword held
rigid before me. The blade broke and I crumpled to my
knees. The hoof-beats of the riderless horse receded in the
distance and I crawled down the hill towards the cottage,
still clutching the remnant of the sword in my right hand.
Only when I got to the doorway did I feel strong enough

to stand up. And it was then I saw that the left side of my shirt was soaked with blood. I staggered further into the room, fearful of what I might find. But the man in the chair was no longer the terrified, stricken figure with gaping mouth and staring eyes. Bentik was, very comfortably, asleep.

I took off my shirt and bathed the wound. As I leaned over the white enamel basin with its blue rim, drops of blood expanded like puffs of smoke in the cold water. And I was trembling. My whole body was shaking with uncontrollable pulses which rocked me from head to foot. I had *done* it! The feeling of exultation swelled in my throat. I had been there when I was needed and I had done it. Faced the demon. Stood in for the banished fugitive and thwarted the vengeful Prince of Verona. I'd earned the right to cry – as Mercutio cries when he is wounded – 'A plague o' both your houses!' It was for those few, fearful, exhilarating minutes on the moor that I'd been summoned. The joy of it was that I'd obeyed the summons without question, though I did not know who needed me, nor why. Standing over the basin with a wet cloth pressed to my shoulder I allowed the excitement of the event to ebb away. But the satisfaction remained – and remains.

Soon, of course, I had to deal with the wound. And I found it impossible to bandage. The deep cut was high on the left side of my chest. Winding the bandage over my shoulder and under my armpit did not quite cover the area. Next I tried winding it completely round my body and snug under both armpits. That was too low. Finally I folded the bandage into a thick pad, placed it in position then lay on top of it, relying on the weight of my body to staunch the blood. And that seemed to work, for I fell asleep in that position and when I woke the bleeding had stopped.

It was Bentik who woke me, but he did not do so until he had prepared breakfast for both of us. And he had shaved. In fact, he seemed quite remarkably elated. There were changes in the room, too. While he strapped my injury with lengths of adhesive tape I looked around. There was no trace of the broken sword, nor of the clasps which had held it above the fireplace. To cover the outline of where it had been he'd brought out a painting which had hung in his bedroom. The Hirschfeld original of Mercutio was gone, as were several photographs of various *Romeo and Juliet* productions.

This clearance of the painful past gave me my cue. Since Bentik had not alluded to the previous night, I didn't either. It was not, of course, that he had forgotten the terrible events. Rather, that his particular tragedy was over. The curtain, at last, had come down on the action which had started onstage in Bucharest. And when a play is fully played to the end the characters have nothing further to say about the action. There are no such lines provided for them.

After breakfast, though – when Bentik insisted on tramping off to the nearest phone to call a doctor – I did venture out and up the hill to the spot where the horse-man had fallen. The broken blade of the sword stuck out of the ground almost vertically. I prised it loose. In bright daylight it was not surprising that there was no blood on the tip. And with the tip I gouged out a narrow trench in which I buried this only remnant of the weapon.

The doctor, as I've said, formed the adamant opinion that my wound was a sub-cutaneous lesion which then split the skin. That was after he'd had me in to his surgery for closer examination. It would have given me great safisfaction if I could have produced my shirt with an open gash at the shoulder but, of course, that was something else Bentik had disposed of before I woke late in the morning. And, in any case, he agreed with the doctor. Part of the astonishing change in him was a newly espoused and gullible belief in modern medicine. During the weeks that followed, he submitted himself to various tests and accepted assurances that there were drugs which could control his epilepsy with perfect safety. He wrote to me saying, 'After all, it's no more awkward than being a diabetic.' That seemed to me awkward enough but undoubtedly it was better than hiding in terror out in the wilderness.

Kenneth Ireland wrote to me as well. For, of course, on my way south after that visit I called in at the Festival Theatre to report on what had happened. And then, also, I suggested to him that it might be worth employing Bentik. He was willing to accept the recommendation and when casting the very next season sent out an invitation.

In later years, the excellent actor did a lot of fine work at Pitlochry, Perth and Dundee. As a matter of fact, he eventually played the part I'd written for him, when a revival was staged in Scotland. He did it under a new stage name; more, I think, to confuse the Inland Revenue than to confound the Prince of Verona. It was ironic that he was not very successful in the custom-made role. But then he'd changed a lot. He'd developed many admirable qualities, but the Mercutio quality had quite gone from him.

However, in Kenneth Ireland's first letter to me after the events I've been describing, he enclosed a cutting from the *Perthshire Advertiser*. I was amazed to discover that my encounter on the moor had been observed by an independent witness. I have the cutting still and I quote it verbatim:

MIDNIGHT DUEL

Kinloch Rannoch farmworker Dugald Thorne (34) stumbled upon a weird duel last Thursday. On the way home from a visit to his fiancée at Blackwater he saw a fight to the finish on the moor. Dugald says, 'There was a man on foot with a sword and he was fighting a man on a horse. He was running and dodging and shouting and trying to defend himself with the sword. I couldn't hear what the man was shouting but he seemed to get the worst of it. He was knocked down and then he disappeared.' Our reporter put on his armour and headed for the jousting site. There were no survivors.

I took some comfort from that report. Whereas Dugald Thorne does not say he saw the horseman, he knew by the attitude and action that I was fighting a horseman. And he knew that I did not just fall down. I was *knocked* down. That is the most significant observation. The fact of my

112

disappearance is accounted for in that I crawled over the crest of the rise and downhill on my hands and knees. To anyone watching from some distance away that would mean disappearing. And from the same vantage point the cottage would be hidden from view. So I think the farmworker is to be trusted, though I cringe at the facetiousness of the newspaper reporter. Kenneth added a dry comment on it, which is also a fair commentary on the whole affair. In his tiny, meticulous handwriting along the margin of the cutting, was quoted a famous line of Romeo's – 'He jests at scars, that never felt a wound.'

For myself, I continue to see productions of the play. And even with the best companies, few will deny that it does fall apart after the banishment. The trouble is, the young lovers kill themselves for no good reason since, in my opinion, Tybalt had it coming to him.

Personal Effects

Frankly – and I don't know how much of it you can take – this story is all about reality and illusion. To my great annoyance at the time, they refused to hold their separate places. Not that I minded the illusion. That, to me, is a very practical commodity from which I earn a living. The trouble was the intrusion of *reality* when I was busy with more important things. So, for a couple of months, I had to jump constantly between one and the other. And it was all my agent's fault.

The theatrical agent always has to know where the client is because a great project may come up at any moment which requires agreement in principle that very day. The client – or *this* client, at least – is less charmed by urgency. I remember too many sudden agreements which ran out of principle when they came to contract and languished, sometimes for years, on the shoals of acrimony.

However, my agent in London did know I was spending three months in New York on a revival and thought nothing of telling my family where I could be found. He also told a personnel manager of a shipping company that, as nominated 'next-of-kin', the personal effects could be delivered to me at West 67th Street. Later he tried to justify this lapse by saying he never gave out such information unless it was a matter of life or death. And this, clearly, was a matter of death.

The apartment was leased to a friend of mine who was off on a European tour. He was a baritone with the Metropolitan Opera. If he'd been a tenor his apartment would have been much nearer Central Park. However, even at the unfashionable end, it was a comfortable hide and within easy walking distance of the Lincoln Center. But there was absolutely no need to go out until rehearsals actually started. Before that, I had two clear months in which to adapt my play, *The Parole of Don Juan*, for a thrust stage and an American cast. The play had originally been written for a traditional proscenium or 'picture frame' raised stage. With a thrust stage the audience is on three sides of the acting area and there is no curtain. Judging by previous experience I would need all of two months to adapt the material.

But it was a job I expected to yield great satisfaction. Most theatre people in New York are an exacting joy to deal with; and crassly professional. One senses there is nothing else they ever wanted to do but work in the theatre and if you don't share that obsession you should get out of the business and look for cleaner work. This is enormously refreshing after London – where the serious theatre is dominated by Cambridge academics who commandeered the stage only when thwarted by lack of ability in other careers.

There I was, then, early in March, settling in for a spell of concentrated work. I was stimulated by the vitality of the city and reassured by the range and efficiency of the personal services available in Manhattan, twenty-four hours a day. It makes an ideal location for a hermit who enjoys comfort. Everything you need or want will come to you.

Also some things you don't want – like a large polished wooden box. For my selective seclusion was invaded by D.J. Lafayette. The doorman buzzed up to say the guy was waiting there and wouldn't take 'No' for an answer. Since 'No' was the only answer I'd told the doorman to give anyone not on my list, I told him to give it again.

'Guy says, you're the next-of-kin and he's gotta see ya,' the doorman's voice crackled in my ear. 'He's got a *box*.'

This startled me. 'What *size* of box?'

'You better see him, Mr Murray. This is official business.'

'Okay. Send him up.'

I glanced at my watch. The person I expected to see that morning was the set-designer for the play I was adapting. He'd sent me a note explaining he'd be briefly in the city and wanted to take the opportunity of putting some ideas to me. However, my first caller was Mr Lafayette, and when he arrived he certainly *looked* as though he was attending official business, if not an actual funeral. He was a dark-haired, rather podgy man with sad eyes. And he did have a box. It was much smaller than a coffin. No larger than a medium-sized suitcase, in fact, though of polished wood and with gleaming metal corner plates.

'Mr Howard Murray?' he enquired.

'Yes. Come in.'

The box must have been heavy because he set it down immediately and turned to face me. 'I've been trying to call you, but your phone seems to be out of order.'

I showed him the receiver lying neatly on the desk-top beside the instrument. 'No, it isn't. I keep it off the hook most of the time.'

He seemed fascinated by this evidence of perversion. 'Why is that, Mr Murray?'

'So the bell doesn't ring when people call me.' I smiled. 'Every now and then, of course, I put it back to calm the phone company's blaster, but mainly it's out of use unless *I* am using it.'

He looked at me warily and sought reassurance. 'You are Howard Murray, the English playwright?'

'Correct in all particulars. Please sit down.' He did so. 'And you are?'

He reached into his waistcoat pocket in order, I thought, to produce his card. But instead he flashed a little identification folder which bore his photograph. I took it from him and read that he was, indeed, D.J. Lafayette, Asst Personnel Manager, The Oregal Shipping Company, Jersey City. Three people who knew him – though I didn't know *them* – had signed to say so. Returning the testimonial I asked, 'When did you have that photograph taken, Mr Lafayette?'

'At Oregal we have them done every five years.'

'Very wise.' I sat opposite him. 'Now. What did you want to see me about?'

116

'Well, sir, first of all to offer my condolences on the loss of Bernard. And then to deliver to you his personal effects.' He tapped the edge of the polished box.

'Bernard who?' I asked.

Lafayette was obviously offended by my callousness but tried not to allow any censure into this voice. 'Bernard Cunningham, chief steward on our *Vogelsund*. As you know, he was reported missing a couple of months ago and is now presumed drowned.'

'Pardon me, Mr Lafayette, I know nothing of the kind.'

The man's fingers tensed on his knees as he caught the first whiff of what could be a departmental foul-up. Immediately he was defensive. 'Notification *was* cabled to your agent in London,' he asserted – guessing.

I could tell he was guessing, but caught him on the hop again by asking, 'Why?'

The answer to that was so obvious he couldn't think of it right away.

I helped him out. 'Mr Lafayette, I do not know, nor to the best of my recollection have I ever known, anyone called Bernard Cunningham.'

We sat silently gazing at each other for a few moments, then, in a commendable effort to regain some of his aplomb, the official looked around and tossed in an available remark he'd meant to use earlier. 'Nice apartment you got here.' After a further pause he added, 'Can I use your telephone?'

'Certainly. I'll warm it up for you,' Replacing the receiver, I noticed he was giving me that mildly hunted look again. I explained 'When it's been off the hook a while, and survived the blaster, it seems to lose interest in normal functioning. Better let it adjust for a couple of minutes.'

He gave it thirty seconds then got through to his office. To save him further embarrassment I went into the bedroom and waited while his voice grew more and more antagonistic. Apparently he was working his way down the chain of command. Getting to the bottom of it, in fact. When he hung up, I rejoined him.

'Well? Have you got it all sorted out?'

He faced me defiantly and his sad eyes had a cunning

gleam. 'All but one thing, Mr Murray. Can you offer me proof of *your* identity?'

'I can, but why should I?'

The thought of having to lug that awkward, heavy box all the way back to Jersey City made him cautious of alienating me further. He smiled 'Well ... as a matter of formality, when I report back I gotta be sure I really saw who I saw. What I mean is, Mr Murray, I've gotta be sure you *are* Howard Murray.' To mitigate the offence of this he added lamely, 'I don't go to the theatre much.'

'Nor do I! However, credit card companies don't care about that.' I opened a drawer of the desk and laid out an array. 'Nor does my bank. And here is some correspondence from my agent. He *does* go to the theatre a lot – but only because he has to.'

The last item satisfied him. 'Ah, your agent.' He pointed triumphantly as though I had trapped myself. 'That's the address!'

'It certainly is.'

He faced me soberly. 'I mean that's the address in our files – and I've checked. Bernard Cunningham's next-of-kin is Howard Murray, *care of* that address.'

'Yes?' It seemed to me we were back exactly where we'd started and I couldn't understand why he seemed so much happier with the situation this time round. 'If that weren't my agent's address, you wouldn't have been able to find *me*. Maybe the stuff should have gone there.'

'It has *been* there. Our Southampton office took it there *and* sent it back.'

'I see. So Bernard Cunningham wasn't lost on the Hudson?'

'No. The Antilles.' He gave me a glance to check my geography and added, 'In the Caribbean.'

'What nationality was this steward?'

'English,' said Lafayette.

'Ah! Then I expect he gave you his home address when he signed on with Oregal.'

'Of course.' He hauled a bundle of documents from the inside pocket of his jacket. 'The address he gave was in London. Lupus Street, SW 1.'

'Pimlico,' I said.

'Yeah. Well, there's nobody there knows him. Of course, we didn't actually check there till he was dead.'

That seemed very reasonable to me. 'And then you tried to deliver the box to my agent.'

'Our Southampton office did. In fact, these particular effects have crossed the Atlantic three times already.' Lafayette sighed and noticeably relaxed his stance. He spelled out the essentials as though to a fractious child. 'Mr Murray, my job is to deliver the personal effects, *personally*, to the next-of-kin; and get a receipt.' He delved into another pocket. 'I have the receipt form right here.'

'I see you have.'

He laid it on the desk. 'Will you sign it, please, and I'll give you the key for the cabinet.'

The word diverted my attention. 'Is that what you call it?'

He was willing to be friendly, now he had the upper hand. 'That's what we call it.' He glanced at the object approvingly. 'Other companies toss everything into burlap but we make a special effort.'

'It *is* very well made,' I said.

'Yeah. Expensive, though.'

I nodded. 'Still, you don't have to provide that many. Or do you?'

'No. Not many.' He tapped the receipt form. 'So – if you don't mind, Mr Murray…'

'Doesn't it matter that I've no idea who Bernard Cunningham is?'

The official conceded, 'That is unusual, but I've…'

'Checked?'

'Yeah. And the important thing is, Bernard Cunningham knew who *you* were. Just like a will, Mr Murray. I guess you're the beneficiary. All he had is in the cabinet – far as we know.' He tapped the form again. 'If you don't mind?'

I signed the form. Lafayette witnessed it, then handed me the key. That accomplished, and when he was just about to leave, his attention flickered again to the telephone. I noticed that he'd inadvertently replaced the receiver on the cradle and quickly removed it.

'You could get a flashing light,' he suggested, 'if you don't like to hear it ring.'

119

'It's not the ringing I mind so much, it's the arbitrary interruption.' Since he seemed fascinated by the subject I added, 'In London, people who must talk to me on the phone send me a note saying exactly when they propose to call. I don't mind that in the least.'

He gave me a tentative smile. 'Great,' he said, and left.

When the door was closed I turned to look at the mysterious 'cabinet' sitting diagonally across a shag-pile cream rug in front of the couch. I had no urge to open it right away but just stared at the impassively glossy side which reflected the chromed legs of the magazine rack. It was then just after noon and time for me to brew some coffee.

While I was waiting, the lure of the cabinet drew me into the living room and I circled the object. The thought occurred to me that as long as it remained unopened its potential was unlimited, and I was unwilling to waste the possibilities of speculation. Here, apparently, was all that remained accessible of Bernard Cunningham. Or, Bernard Cunningham as the personnel officer had called him. Wherever the stress fell, I'd certainly never heard of him. Chief steward on a general-cargo boat, the *Vogelsund*. That was scarcely a career. Indeed, it was the sort of job which could be obtained, if not held, without competence. The sort of job that young men running away to sea might settle for. But how would this incompetent runaway know of *me*? It was clear he merely knew *of* me or he would have got a closer address than my agent. But that just made the whole thing more puzzling. If he didn't know me personally, why on earth should he choose me as his next-of-kin?

That term is so much in use one tends to be ignorant of its meaning. And dictionaries are no help. They, too trustingly, believe that it means a family relationship. But, as Hamlet scathingly muttered about his stepfather, that's 'A little more than kin, and less than kind'. So, I was on Bernard Cunningham's side when he ordained that he was the best judge of who his kin might be. Of course, there would have been no difficulty at all about the matter if the official form had required the next-of-kith. A total stranger can never be *kith*.

120

Bernard, I felt sure, must have had some kith. Why hadn't he promoted one of them? I went back into the kitchen, poured myself coffee, then sat down opposite the gleaming box. It showed no obvious sign of having travelled the Atlantic three times, but perhaps the contents had been repacked in a new cabinet before they were delivered to me. And it was time to discover what the contents were. The key turned easily in the little solid brass locks and I swung the lid back so that it lay flat on the rug.

The interior of the cabinet was divided irregularly into several compartments. The largest of these was packed with clothes. I spread them out on the couch. There were several light-coloured tee-shirts and two more formal shirts with frilled jabots, three highly coloured blouson jackets, two pairs of denim jeans and two pairs of white slacks. The underwear was red and the briefs looked no more supportive than posing pouches. There were also several pairs of nylon socks, a pair of canvas shoes and a pair of leather moccasins.

In other compartments of the cabinet were: an electric shaver, a travelling clock, a small portable radio, three pairs of sunglasses, a Polaroid camera and several photographs of different cheerful and pretty girls – two of them naked. An inset box contained 150 US dollars and an inventory supplied by the shipping company listing all these contents. An appendix noted the uniform and overalls supplied to Bernard Cunningham, but did not state how many of those items had been reclaimed.

I sat back and surveyed the surprising cargo which had been delivered into my care. Gradually my sense of irritation turned to downright annoyance. It is annoying to be taken for a fool. And the contents of the box suggested that somebody thought me very foolish indeed. For it was immediately obvious that Bernard Cunningham was *not* dead. It puzzled me that the shipping company had been so hasty in presuming he'd drowned.

The doorman's buzzer sounded again. The designer had arrived. My first impulse was to gather up and hide all the clothes which I'd strewn over the couch but then the idea occured to me that exactly the expert I needed for my

121

enquiries was on his way up in the elevator. He was a young man who'd recently returned from t.v. slumming in California where he'd been employed designing costumes for a popular soap opera. It was his intention to make the Lincoln Center pay dearly for his loss of virtue.

Actually, he should not have come to see me on his own, but he hoped to steal a march on the director of the piece. If he could get me to approve his preliminary outlines 'in principle' he'd thus pre-empt what the director might prefer. I'd no intention of letting him do that. And before we even got to *The Parole of Don Juan* I wanted him to 'cast' Bernard Cunningham from his costumes.

I invited him to suppose we were casting a modern, very realistic play.

'Yeah?' He eyed the haberdashery and nodded, willing to humour me for the moment, so that I'd more readily agree with him later.

'But this time we're going to start with the costumes *then* hire an actor that they'd suit.'

He grinned. 'Seems to me an ideal method for casting a play.'

'Yes. I thought it would appeal to you. In fact – to take it further – this time the costumes determine what the play will be about.'

'Even better!'

'So. I want you to examine the costumes spread over the couch there. Then describe to me the man who would wear them.'

Apart from his wish to keep me in a good mood, I could tell the designer was genuinely fascinated by the problem I'd set him. First he examined the slacks, assessing the length of leg, the taper, the waistband and the stitching. Briskly he snapped one pair inside-out to look closely at the silk inserts around the crotch. He held the frilled shirts up to the light then concentrated on how they'd been cut under the arms. The socks, briefs and sneakers were impatiently dismissed but the tee-shirts were inspected around the neck-band and at the arm-bands. Finally he devoted some time to the leather moccasins before turning to me with a smile. 'Okay,' he said. 'Ask.'

'What age is he?'

'I'd say mid-twenties.'

'Height and weight?'

'Five foot ten, six foot. About 160 pounds. He's a slim guy, but he has heavy shoulders. The slacks give him a neat waist but you need shoulders for the blousons. Also, stretched armbands on the tee-shirts make him pretty heavy on top.'

'That seems fairly conclusive.'

'I can tell you his complexion. Swarthy – or good permanent tan. Nobody with a pale skin would wear so much light colour, or white. What's more, he's a pretty expensive dresser and "in". You got there Italian slacks.' He picked up a pair and laid the legs over his forearm. 'Tapered. And cuffs. They're just coming in again.'

'Italian? But I looked at the labels. They were bought in London.'

'Sure. A franchise deal. But only the Italians worry so much about trapping their pubic hair.' He drew my attention to the silk inserts at the inner fork and fly of the trousers. 'And with those briefs ...' he pointed to the discarded red cotton pouches '... that's a problem.'

'Anything else?'

'The moccasins are Italian too. He has broad feet and he likes dancing. Also, he wears a *chain* earring in his left ear – the threads are drawn in the neckbands of the tee-shirts.'

'Excellent. Now, who are we going to cast for these clothes?'

'First, you set the play in a warm climate,' said the designer. 'Then what we need is an easy-going, good-looking guy ... a bit vain, maybe ... who's not short of a dollar. Likes to impress the gals – and probably does.' He shrugged. 'A *modern* Don Juan, could be.'

Whether he said that because he wanted to remind me of our proper business or because it seemed apt, I didn't know. But certainly it was time we got down to business. He unpacked the bundle of large sketches he'd prepared for the proposed set and costumes and spread them out on the floor. Neither of us had worked in the Vivian Beaumont Theater before and, as things turned out, it was unlikely *he* would again. However, I listened to what he

123

said and looked at his sketches and made as little comment as possible.

It was when he came to the costume designs that I had to object. In the play, Don Juan is released from hell to have another go at his life; to mend his profligate ways and generally reform. This parole is achieved through the intercession of the Danish philosopher, Søren Kierkegaard, who'd always been on the best of terms with God and gets leave of absence from Heaven to act as the Spaniard's parole officer.

The designer had shown the two principals in correct period dress; that is, seventeenth century Spain and nineteenth century Denmark respectively, but he'd illustrated Kierkegaard as a tall, slim and elegant figure with a cane.

'That won't do,' I said.

The designer looked up with a smile in place, but decidedly cool eyes. 'Why not?'

'Kierkegaard was a hunchback.'

The young man gulped. 'What!'

I nodded. 'Saintly, but a hunchback.'

There was a pause then the designer said, 'I never read anything about that.' His voice strengthened in defence of his sketch. 'It doesn't say *that* in any of the reference books I looked at. How come?'

'Perhaps the people who wrote the reference books didn't think it relevant – or they just didn't know.'

He gathered up the sketches which were spread out across the rug. 'Well – if it's not relevant why mention it?'

'It may not be relevant in reference books but I would have thought it essential information for you.'

'I don't see how it is, Mr Murray.' He was digging himself in.

'Of course it is. Think of casting. There must be very few leading actors who are natural hunchbacks – even in New York. So, it will be your job to provide the hump; in the costume. You'll also have to provide an umbrella, not a cane. Søren never went *any*where without his umbrella.'

The young designer leapt to his feet angrily. 'I don't see it makes any difference. All this is too … *special*.'

'Not *too* special. And it does make a difference. There is

124

a crucial difference between your upright, slender young man flourishing his cane and a middle-aged, unkempt, hunchback who is terrified of getting wet. One is a nonentity and the other has the most beautiful mind that Europe produced in the whole of the nineteenth century.'

As he headed for the door he said, 'I design beautiful costumes, not beautiful minds.'

I reminded him, 'But you're not doing soap now. Into each life *some* rain must fall.'

He slammed out.

I shook my head at the pointlessness of the temper. If he got angry enough, would that make me *wrong*? If he slammed a door in modern New York, would the shock straighten Kierkegaard's back or dim by a fraction his brilliance? It is my conviction that, in the theatre, if you know the truth you should tell the truth. And on the rare occasions where reality is any help at all, you should use that as well.

I started repacking everything in the box as near as possible to the way I'd received it. As an afterthought I removed the shipping company's inventory then locked the cabinet and slid it under the couch out of sight. That done, I sat back, lit a cigarette and reflected on my contention that Bernard Cunningham – about whom I now knew a great deal more – was not dead. Surely that must have been obvious to whoever made up the inventory. These personal effects had been edited *before* they were listed. Bernard had *chosen* what he would leave with the same care as he'd chosen the person to whom he would leave it.

The first striking deficiency was the lack of any photograph showing Bernard. What fashion-conscious young man does not keep photographs of himself? There should also have been shipboard photographs of Bernard and his mates – with the mates rather in the background, I fancied. Next, there were no letters. That was a particularly glaring fault in someone I took to be a poor correspondent. Such people are always putting off answering letters, and thus keep what is sent to them against the day when they get round to the chore of replying. Good correspondents, on the other hand, keep not only what is sent to them but copies of what they send. There were no letters at all because letters would contain addresses. Finally – and most damning – there was no rubbish. Few, if any, of us were we snatched off the world all unprepared, could boast that we left absolutely no detritus of living. Unwisely, Bernard had been over-tidy in his preparation.

I got up and went to stand by the well-heated window, staring down at the street, ten floors below. It occurred to me that I should call Mr Lafayette to tell him what he should have been able to see for himself, but decided that would be unsporting. It would mean betraying a confidence; even though I was not meant to be in possession of that confidence. Unless, of course, Bernard was much more intelligent than I gave him credit for.

It was *possible* he'd expected me to make the deduction I had made; that he'd wanted everyone else to believe he was dead but had wanted me to know he was alive. Why? Even if that were the case, what purpose could it serve? Certainly no purpose of mine. Of his, then? He'd imposed an obligation upon me, without my knowledge. But I had accepted it. My possession of the cabinet and its contents could be a lever in some mysterious con. Yet, as far as I knew, I'd done nothing illegal. Lafayette had assured me it was okay. He'd checked.

In the street, the late afternoon traffic was beginning to build up, most of it heading west from the Central Park transverse and from Broadway too. It is much easier to get into the Upper West Side than it is to get out if you live in New Jersey. I glanced at the letterhead of the inventory. Oregal's office was in Jersey City but the wharf they used was further south on the Upper Bay, at Bayonne.

And that was the number I called to enquire about the next date of arrival for the *Vogelsund*. It wasn't due back there for a couple of weeks. I asked if a berthing detail had been allocated and thus learned the precise time at which the crew would come ashore.

It seemed to me likely that even if Bernard had arranged his own disappearance he must have had help aboard the ship. There must be someone else who knew he hadn't drowned in the Caribbean. I murmured to myself,

126

'Though, if you're thinking of drowning, that's the place to do it.'

Two weeks later, at 6.30 a.m., I was standing in a cold drizzle on the Bayonne wharf. The freighter had just berthed but none of the crew was showing much sign of coming ashore. Probably they intended to have breakfast first. People spend far too much time eating. I pulled the deep collar of my overcoat higher around my ears and gazed out at the bay. On the far side, the Port of Brooklyn lights were veiled strands of yellow and blue. To the south, the Verrazano Bridge was no more than a spectral sketch for an impossible feat of engineering. To the north, the Statue of Liberty was completely hidden by curtains of fine rain.

I cursed the weather for, as part of my dishevelled look, I was not wearing a hat. Normally, winter or summer, I carry or wear a hat. And the coat was getting waterlogged. It was a long and ancient navy-blue velour coat which I'd bought specially for the occasion in a 24th Street thrift shop as a sort of buddy-can-you-spare-a-dime costume. Even in dry weather it would have seen too much service. But the steady rain – though decidedly uncomfortable – was a bonus. It plastered my hair flat in lank, dirty-looking strands and made the coat sag at the seams.

Now there was some movement on deck and the other people waiting drew closer to the security fence which kept us about a hundred yards from the gangway. They didn't look as though they were meeting anyone off the ship. This was a humdrum occasion and they were there to start work on the turn-around. No effort would be spared to make that operation as speedy as possible. A working ship in harbour is not only failing to make money, it is actually losing money. So the turn-around mateys had to prove themselves raring to go.

I rehearsed my plan of action. Nothing would be achieved if I just stopped the first person to come ashore, particularly if he was alone. By the time I'd explained my business, and he'd told me he couldn't help, everyone else would have passed by. The thing was to stop an apt-looking man who was in a group. They'd probably wait for him and he could apply to them for information, thus increasing my chances of success. It was a trick I'd learned from Coleridge. His delightful old loony is crafty enough to stop one of *three* wedding guests. And that one turned out to be next-of-kin, as well. So it was important to choose the right group. First to leave, I reckoned, would be the deck officers who were free of duty. Then would come the engineers. Finally, the more casual crewmen and the galley staff who'd have to clear up *after* breakfast. And they'd be the men likely to know about a missing steward.

What I had in mind was very simple. If I was to be involved in a con I wanted to give them the opportunity to put on the bite. That would be easier to recognise than the bait, and might give me some idea of how I was to be used and what was to be gained at my expense. Probably there would be money involved to extricate myself from some legal nicety hidden in the elaborate charade. In any event, if there was some trick to be played, now was the time for somebody else to make a move. I was giving them the chance to show but, in my appearance, warning them of slim pickings.

As it happened, nobody left on his own because they all intended to share cabs. By the time the mess complement swung off the gangway I was beginning to have doubts about my strategy, but it paid off. As the bunch of young men, all in high spirits and wearing casual clothes, came nearer I called out, 'Bernard! Bernard Cunningham?' Their stride faltered and I saw them glance at each other. I moved in and repeated the enquiry. 'Bernard?' They stopped.

'Bernard isn't here,' one of them said.

'Isn't this the *Vogelsund*?'

'Sure! You got the *Vogelsund* okay, but Bernard is...'

One of his colleagues interrupted him sharply. 'Just a minute.' The others drew back a little to let him speak to me directly. My accent, evident myopia and general air of helplessness was creating the illusion that I was a relative of the deceased who hadn't been 'told'. The man who undertook that sad duty was stocky and had crinkly fair hair. 'You from England?' he asked.

'Yes. I'm looking for Bernard Cunningham.'

'He's not with us, mister. You better ask at the office up in Jersey.'

'Is he there?' I asked.

'No. But they'll tell you about ... what happened.'

'Aw! You tell him, Bruno,' an impatient friend suggested.

'Tell me what?'

Bruno hunched his shoulders abruptly. 'He was lost at sea. Happened coupla months ago. They shoulda told ya. Sorry.'

Since there was no time to waste in bad news assimilation I jumped several stages to the main question. 'Did you know him?'

Bruno nodded. 'Sure. He was a good friend of mine. We shared a cabin.'

That was the first thing I wanted to know. 'Thank you for telling me Mr...?'

'Caplow.'

And that was the second thing. 'Mr Caplow.'

'Bruno! Come on!' protested an older man who was anxious to get away.

Bernard's friend took his hand out of his pocket and tapped my upper arm with the side of his fist. 'Sorry you heard this way. You his uncle?'

'I ... I'm...' A little emotional blockage stopped me.

'They shoulda told you, at the office. You go see them, anyways.'

With that, all of them wheeled in close formation and headed for the dock exit. I watched them go with satisfaction. Bruno Caplow, pronounced Chaploff, was going to find me more persistent than this brief meeting allowed. And now, too, I had an uncle to conjure with. As I walked slowly between the acres of condemned-looking warehouses it occurred to me that it must be an uncle on the mother's side or Bruno would have called me Mr Cunningham. It could be, of course, he knew I was an impostor. Maybe that was why he *hadn't* put the bite on. That must be tested the next time we met. The test came sooner than I expected.

When I got to the access road there was only one cab left. I signalled and, when it drew up, Bruno Caplow

129

already had possession. He wound down the window and asked, 'You want the Holland Tunnel?'

'Yes,' I said. 'That would suit me fine.'

He threw open the door and I got in.

'It was kind of you to wait for me.'

'Least I could do,' the young man said.

As the cab snaked north through the blurred landscape, I calculated that the next question should be his. If he thought me a genuine relative he'd want to know why I'd been kept ignorant of Bernard's death. In answer to that I was prepared to confess hopeless alcoholism. If he thought me an impostor he probably knew who I really was and we could get things straight. He offered neither of these gambits. Instead, and somewhat to my embarrassment, he started lamenting the loss of his friend. 'Me an' Bern had some great times,' he said. 'I sure miss him. A lot. Real hell-raiser, Bern was.'

'Was he?'

'Before he got religion, I mean. We were real close buddies then. Even after, he was still a guy ya could trust.'

'I'm glad to hear that, Bruno.'

'An' it cut both way. There was nothin' he woun't do for me either.'

It struck me that Bruno had been waiting for the opportunity to tell this to somebody. Presumably such recollections would not readily fit his day to day contacts with his other shipmates but it was all right to be honest with a relative of the dead man. And that was unsettling. For Bruno evidently believed that his friend was dead. My conviction that Bernard was still alive began to falter. What was expected of me right at that moment, though, was some affectionate recollection of my nephew which I was not able to offer. 'It's all very sad,' I said.

'Whaddya want to see Bernard *about*?' he asked. 'Maybe I could help.'

I decided to jump in with both feet. 'He owed me money.'

Apparently, this did not surprise Bruno. 'Much?'

'A lot for me.'

'Take it up with his mother.'

I pitched my response somewhere between hopeless

creditor and disowned relative. 'They don't tell me anything. I don't know where she is, now.'

He turned almost completely round to stare at me. 'You don't *know*?'

'Do you?'

'London. She's in London. How come you don't know that?'

I shrugged. 'London's a big place.'

He expelled breath in an impatient gust. 'Chrissakes, mister – if ya can find the right man on the right ship, clear off the ocean into B*ayonne*, you sure as hell can find your sister in your own home town.'

I tried hard to suppress a smile. Bruno had hit upon the weakest point of my role. And it seemed this evidence of my futility ruled out any further interest he might have in my plight. The cab swept into the maw of the Holland Tunnel and we stared straight ahead in silence as the regular flash of lights held us in strobed immobility.

However reluctantly, I had to admit to myself that there was not going to be a bite. And perhaps there was no con. Or, if there was a con, Bruno Caplow was not part of it. He'd given me some more information but it didn't lead anywhere. Nor was his attitude in the least suspect. He was willing to help and not afraid to confess affection. But suppose all this was part of the act. I decided to give him one last chance. 'My name's Howard Murray,' I said.

'Glad to know ya, Howard.' He shook my hand perfunctorily and waited for the daylight of Manhattan to appear. Once out of the tunnel he seemed to cheer up a little. 'I catch the local for Queens,' he told me and I deduced he'd be doing the longest part of his journey home by subway. He got out at 14th Street and paid for the first stage, including the toll and excluding any contribution from me. I gave him a wave but waited until he was out of earshot before saying where I wanted to go. The driver was none too happy about taking a drenched, middle-aged bum all that way uptown so I showed him I had more than enough money to pay the fare.

I tried to put Bernard Cunningham out of my mind and

concentrated on work. Other productions off-Broadway, then at the ANTA Playhouse, had taught me the necessity of adapting my English dialogue for American actors – a necessity which most English writers ignore. But the fact is, there is a great difference in style from one side of the Atlantic to the other. To generalise (and oversimplify) the difference is that English actors are talking heads who move and American actors are moving bodies who talk. One has only to recall some disastrous productions of American plays at the English National Theatre to realise the discrepancy cuts both ways.

The Parole of Don Juan has a good many long speeches, and that was where careful reworking was needed. American actors are shorter of breath than English actors. That meant rephrasing. But more important is the *shape*. An English actor will deliver a long speech in straight well-varied lengths of sentences and phrases, and the shape is all outside his mouth. From a New Yorker it comes like fruit peel. It's a continuous sliver of varying width and thickness which is curved and coloured and you can tell from any section of it exactly what is *inside* being peeled. Such a process disguises the fact that the speech has been written at all. And that's fine with me. Customers don't go to the theatre to see plays. They go to see performances.

Deliberations of this sort were interrupted a couple of days later by the return of Lafayette. He gave my uncradled telephone a fierce look – from which I concluded he'd been trying to call me again – then told me straight, 'We've had a letter from Mrs Cunningham.'

'She wants the personal effects?'

'No. She doesn't know about that.'

'That's very strange,' I said. 'Surely you let her know?'

'Mr Murray, there was no way we *could* let her know. As far as we knew Bernard wasn't married.'

To prevent the cross-purposes becoming too entangled I asked, 'May I see the letter?'

'Sure.' He was more casually dressed on this occasion, but still all his pockets were bulging.

I took the sheet of azure-tinted notepaper which bore a printed sticker identifying the sender as Mrs B. Cunningham at an address in Hampstead. It read;

Dear Bernard,

I'm so sorry I wasn't able to get back in time for the Southampton call but the rally in Bradford spilled over to several constituency meetings which were quite *vital* & I was organizing day & night for most of that week – Oh! my poor butt. But let *us* get organised. Do send an up-to-date itinerary. Better still get off that rotten boat and do something useful. Much love, E.

All of this was scrawled across the page at an upward tilt, without paragraphs and leaving no margins. I handed the note back to Lafayette.

He said, 'It seems Bernard's wife doesn't know he was drowned.'

'His mother,' I corrected. 'That's a letter from his mother.' The official slapped his brow. 'Worse yet!'

'When was the *Vogelsund* due in Southampton?'

'The last trip. She just got back. Southampton would be about seven days ago.' He produced an itinerary. 'Yep. March 22 from Hamburg. Sail 23.' He offered the list to me, then stuffed it back in his pocket, wearily shaking his head. 'What do we tell her? You sure it's his mother?' His sharp upward glance suggested things might not be so bad if it were a wife who had to be told. 'Why wouldn't she sign it – "Mother"?'

'Because she's a very busy lady with a career which didn't include being a mother any longer than she had to.' I thought of adding a short homily on Hampstead women who are into politics but doubted if Lafayette would get the picture.

Again he moaned, 'What do we *tell* her?'

'Tell her nothing. Just send her an itinerary.'

Lafayette gawped at me. 'What? We can't do that!'

'Well then, let me write to her.'

A possible way out arrested the droop of his head, but his voice was decently non-committal. 'You, Mr Murray?'

'Yes. Suppose that letter had arrived before you delivered the cabinet to me. You would have included it with the other personal effects, wouldn't you?'

'Yeah. Yeah, sure!' Relief was beginning to break over the troublesome situation.

'So? I'm the person who should have it now.'

Lafayette nodded. 'That's right. That certainly is the case.' He handed me the letter. 'And you'll write to her?'

'Yes, of course,' I lied.

He nodded again, glad to escape from the possible consequences of his department's ham-fistedness. Then, after a few pleasantries, he left.

I tried to resume work but the verbal duel between Magister Søren Kierkegaard and Don Juan Tenorio in long-ago Seville withdrew, with good grace, to an ante-room of my attention. In their place, steward Bernard Cunningham claimed the follow-spot. What was he up to? And what would he do next? For I was still sure that enlisting me as next-of-kin had a purpose. My involvement with his fake death would be put to some use.

I began to speculate on how my accepting that responsibility could be used. It was possible, for example, that Bernard had large debts as well as inadequate personal effects. Depending on how they were incurred, I could be liable to pay them. Or it was possible that he had substantial life-insurance which would be paid to me and collected by him or by someone else who had better claim to it. My role could be either as a sucker or a patsy, neither of which I relished.

But extorting or re-directing money through a con now seemed less likely. I'd provided the opportunity and it hadn't been taken. Bruno Caplow was contentedly back in Queens with his family, Mr Lafayette in Jersey was satisfied he'd done the right thing and, in London, all Mrs Cunningham wanted was an itinerary. There was no threat from anyone – except from Bernard himself. His was the threat of the inexplicable.

Glancing again at Mrs Cunningham's letter, it occurred to me that the whole plot could be an act of revenge. If my interpretation of the relationship between Bernard and his mother was correct it could be he wanted to demonstrate how her self-centred political activism had lost him. But it had misfired. If she hadn't been so busy in Bradford, she would have met the ship on its most recent call at Southampton. She would then have discovered Bernard wasn't aboard and been told how he drowned in the

134

Caribbean a couple of months earlier. Her frantic enquiries of the shipping company would reveal that they hadn't told her because they didn't know about her. Also, that a complete stranger was designated next-of-kin. All going well, she'd return to Hampstead a sadder and wiser woman, if not absolutely brimming with regret. I smiled to myself on reflecting that she'd been spared all this because she *wasn't* a wiser woman. And I'd every hope of letting her continue to be foolish. It was probably what she did best.

If that scenario was anywhere near the truth, it seemed likely Bernard would wish to be within gloating distance when the tragedy was made known. Revenge must yield personal satisfaction or it can look frustratingly like an accident. It followed, therefore, that he wouldn't remain long, swanning around where he was 'drowned'. The Caribbean is fine for a holiday but its unvarying blandness would soon pall on an energetic young man. Apart from that, Bernard had chosen a next-of-kin who had an address in London. But again the plan (if this *was* the plan) had gone awry. I wasn't where he expected me to be either. There had been no confrontation between the distraught mother and the stranger her son had preferred as recipient of his worldly goods. We'd all missed our cues. '"And where are the clowns?"' I asked myself. '"There ought to be clowns."'

I put the telephone back on its hook, gave it a few minutes' rehabilitation, then called my agent. There was a chance that Bernard had gone where he expected the action to take place. If nothing happened he'd want to know why. It was my intention to rely on what the designer had told me and ask if any young man of that description had made an appearance. But I was fore-stalled. My agent, he *said*, had been just about to call me. A girl had been at the office looking for me. Her name was Tricia Welles. She'd also asked about that box.

'What exactly did she say about the box?'

'She wanted to know if we'd received a box, for you.'

'What did you tell her?' I asked.

'I told her the truth.'

'Remind me what that is.'

There was a pause on the other end of the line as my agent tried to make out if I was in one of my 'difficult' moods or just being playful. He said carefully, 'I told her that a box had been brought here but it was for you on a strictly personal delivery basis so we couldn't accept it.'

'Then she asked where I was.'

'Yes,' he said.

'And you told her.'

'No! No, Howard, I didn't.'

'Good. She didn't leave a phone number, I suppose.'

'Yes, she did. That's what I was going to call you...' There was another pause. 'What?' he asked someone there with him in the office. Then he reported to me, 'She told Janice she's seen your plays.' Janice was his secretary.

'Ah, has she!' I sighed as a new perspective came into focus. 'But she didn't ask where I could be found?'

'No. She just wanted to know where the box was.' There was another whispered aside. 'Janice told her it was being taken back to New York.'

'I see.' Apparently it had not occurred to either of them that if an item which must be personally received was on its way to New York, it must necessarily come to me. My agent gave me the girl's number then, after some talk about how the adaptation was progressing and about a letter he'd had from the Writers Guild in New York (a difficult bunch as always) I hung up.

Now – it was at that point I began to see the light; and if you have read the first story in this book first, maybe you can see it too. For the moment, let me just point out the coincidence of Bernard, Bruno, the dominant mother, the girl and the intervention of a total stranger.

As the pattern began to emerge I was certain that, before I left New York, Bernard Cunningham would come to me. All this was speculation, mind, but such indications as there were demanded another meeting with Bruno Caplow. In the moment of euphoria at a possible solution I suddenly felt hungry. It had been a couple of days since my last full meal so I phoned round to the delivery restaurant which normally supplied me with cooked food and gave them an order to be sent up as soon as ready.

Then I called Lafayette to get Bruno's address and number. The explanation I gave was the same as I intended to give Bruno himself – that Bernard wanted to settle a debt he owed his shipmate and had left some money for the purpose. Lafayette accepted the story and, I thought, Bruno did too. But the *Vogelsund* cook was wary enough to suggest that we meet in a bar and not in his home. He offered no explanation but just stipulated how to get to the chosen bar by subway.

Probably there are very good reasons why not much is written about Queens. All the rags-to-riches stories seem to originate in the Lower East Side, Brooklyn, the Bronx or even Hoboken – which are great places to get out of as fast as you can. Queens exerts no such pressure. And it is no more depressing than the suburbs which separate most international airports from the hub they serve. The only remarkable things is that in Queens cremation must have been outlawed for a long time. Though dressed in my disreputable velour coat, I took the cab. The speed and convenience of the New York subway has never convinced me it's worth all that ugliness.

The bar was a pleasant-looking modern place off Steinway Street, and Bruno was waiting. He bought me a beer and we sat in a corner booth so that I could make the bequest in privacy. However, there was a lot I wanted him to tell me before we got to the money. But my first question did little to reassure him. 'Are you married, Bruno?'

He gave me a hostile stare over his beer. 'What's it to you?' I made no response and waited for an answer. 'Yeah. Sure, I'm married.'

'Was Bernard married?'

'Jees, naw!' He gave a good-humoured grunt at the idea. 'Bernard had no strings.'

'He had a lot of girlfriends, though.'

The cook shrugged his broad shoulders. 'All in the past. Friends they were sometimes, girls always.' He smiled suddenly and shook his head admiringly. 'That guy ...

Jeeze!' He slapped the table. 'That guy could get under any skirt he looked at half steady. They stood in *line* for it.'

Almost involuntarily I remarked, 'A regular Don Juan, eh?'

'Who?'

'What was it about him that attracted them?'

'Mister, I donno, but I ain't got it. He jist looked at them an' kep *lookin'* hard enough to see through them, an' pretty soon he was *jammed* right through them.'

'But then he got religion.'

The light of vicarious conquest died in Bruno's eyes and he sighed. 'Hell, whadda waste!'

'What was it that changed him?'

'Gonorrhoea,' said Bruno flatly. Then added, 'Ya can't put your wick in all that pussy without there's a *risk*.'

'I suppose so. But he was cured, wasn't he?'

'Sure. Of the gunge and the screwin', both.' Bruno shook his head at the injustice of it.

'Did he ever mention a particular girl? At home in England?'

'Yeah, Tricia.'

'Weren't they thinking of getting married?'

'She might have.'

Getting information from Bruno wasn't easy. I prompted him. 'Did you ever meet Tricia?'

'*She*'s the one's after something, huh?'

'You have met her?'

He nodded and turned to look lazily around the dimly lit room. It was early afternoon and there was quite a steady ebb and flow of men having after-lunch or intead-of-lunch drinks. There was very little conversation – a fact which probably commended the place to Bruno. While he kept his eyes on the other customers, he said, 'You say you got some money for me?'

'Yes.' I reached into a deep side pocket of the overcoat. I'd put the 150 dollars from the cabinet into an envelope with Bruno's name on it. 'Not much, but it must must have been some debt he owed you.' I laid the envelope on the table.

Bruno looked at the envelope then squarely into my

138

eyes. 'Bernard did not *ever* owe me anything, Howard.'

I slid the envelope across to him. He slid it right back. I was puzzled. 'Then why did you agree to meet me here?'

'Because I want to know what you are *at*, mister.' There was just the hint of threatening hostility in his voice. 'That's why.'

I now saw my own arrogance. Clearly, I had misjudged Bruno's intelligence and, more crucially, his integrity. That oversight led me to consider telling the truth of what I suspected and hoped to do. But I managed to suppress the impulse. Instead, a better lie. 'I'm trying to get Bernard's mother to sue the company,' I said.

He raised his eyebrows sceptically. 'Don't think it'll work.'

'But I have to know how it happened. How Bernard came to drown.'

Bruno was willing to help me with that, though he couldn't see any reason for blaming the Oregal Shipping Company.

It had happened after a run ashore when they were on the launch taking them back to the ship. Everyone was drunk except Bernard. He'd recently 'got religion', as Bruno put it, and had abandoned his old ways. But he still went out with his friends. He'd practically carried Bruno down to the launch which set out across the bay severely overloaded. It was dark and everybody was horsing around. Bernard moved about, fore and aft, restraining the more foolhardy. All of them remembered that. But when they got to the ship and, one by one, heaved themselves aboard, Bernard was missing. There was none of the shore party who could swear that he hadn't, accidentally, pushed Bernard into the water. The ship lowered its own boats to search around. And they kept searching till well after sunrise.

'So, it wasn't the ship's launch which took you back to the ship?'

'Naw. It was hired – like you'd hire a cab and share the bill.'

I nodded. 'And how far was it from the shore to the ship?'

'Too far to swim,' said Bruno with perceptive intensity.

139

His tone and the flinty expression of his light grey eyes suggested he knew what was really in my mind. Maybe he'd had his own suspicions about the apparent loss of his friend, but that friend could still claim his loyalty. For the first time since I'd got into the bizarre affair I had the feeling of a real person behind it. Bruno, for all his guarded indifference, had cared about Bernard Cunningham and presumably that high opinion had been earned.

As mildly as possible, I asked, 'Did the commercial launch join in the search?'

'No. Didn't have the lights. It was pretty dark out there.' He leaned over the table. 'Ya havena hope in hell to sue *them*, if that's what you're thinkin'.'

I shook my head in agreement, but what I was thinking was that Bernard didn't need to swim ashore. All he had to do was conceal himself in the dark launch until it *returned* him to the shore. In the urgency and confusion of the night it would be easy for him to slip away. Of course that, and everything else, would have been planned beforehand. I was more than ever convinced that Bernard's death was a carefully staged illusion.

As I was driven back through the graveyards of Queens, it seemed to me that Bruno Caplow must have been the nearest Bernard could get to a brother. For, of course, I'd made up my mind that Bernard was an only child. No doubt his mother had arranged things so that the worst of the pregnancy and birth coincided with the long recess of Parliament. I'd also decided that she was a Labour Party worker, though the only evidence I had of that was Hampstead and the fact that she seemed to take politics *seriously*.

A few days later, coming out of the apartment building and walking towards Broadway, I had the clear impression that I was being followed. It's a difficult feeling to be accurate about because it is alerted not by any of the utility senses but by a deeper pressure point which is sensitive to danger – whether there is any likelihood of danger or not. In upper Broadway around the mid-60s on a spring day mugging was unlikely, so I reasoned that the person

140

following me must be Bernard Cunningham. And he wasn't having an easy time of it. Manhattan sidewalks are littered with an array of fixed obstacles. Here, the frontage owners seem able to do what they like; and what they like projects. It's an arrangement which would give English planning authorities hysterics. The profusion of street furniture is concentrated in a Maginot line along the kerb but is augmented by free-standing shop signs, trash cans, basement barriers, awning stanchions, direction plate gantries and cables tangling like spaghetti at every corner. Whatever the height of the buildings, the pedestrian zig-zags through a fairly low tunnel.

I was on my way to the Library of Performing Arts where I hoped to find which of the older theatres still had traditional machinery. I turned west along 65th Street which is one-way and quieter. There, I thought, I'd be able to spot whoever was trailing me. It wasn't a good choice. Outside the Juilliard School of Music there were a lot of young men coming from every direction who fitted the description of Bernard. I quickly crossed the street to the corner with Amsterdam and sought to lose myself in the bustle there. Just as I turned the corner I glanced back and saw a single figure duplicating my actions.

When I went into the library he followed. It might seem that he was inept and clumsy, but of course Bernard was convinced that I'd no idea what he looked like. My first impulse was to approach him directly but I rejected that because there was the possibility that he was indeed a Juilliard student. In my experience, any one of them is more formidable than a whole platoon of inquisitors. That music school produces the toughest, sharpest brains I've ever encountered. Once their interest is aroused nothing can shake them off. I was in no condition for such a workout.

It seemed best to allow him to approach me. If it *was* Bernard that, surely, would be his intention. I gave him every opportunity but he remained stolidly examining the exhibition in the entrance hall. I managed to stop an assistant near him and to her said, 'Excuse me. My name is Howard Murray ...' I did not have to ask for the information. She recognised the name, knew what I was

141

working on and in general gave me a big welcome – all within earshot of the hovering follower. And it seemed that was the positive identification he wanted for he immediately walked out of building. I made use of my time collecting information on the recent use of grave-traps around Times Square.

For those who don't see that many period plays – or traditional theatres, a grave-trap is a hole in the centre of the stage covered by down-swinging trapdoors. Normally, it is six feet long and three feet wide. It is cut lengthwise across the stage at a central position so that the 'mourners' can form a visually satisfying tableau. Burials used to be as popular on the stage as they are in Queens. But dying has gone out of fashion, so modern theatres do not have grave-traps – not even if they cost eight million dollars, like the Vivian Beaumont Theater. Hell is even less fashionable than being buried, but that was what *I* wanted the trap to represent. Don Juan emerges from Hell at the beginning of the play and is dragged down into it by the statue at the end. For that, we needed a grave-trap. But I'd noticed on the designer's sketches of the proposed set that he did *not* propose to have Don Juan rising out of the ground. I had two weeks in which to try different rewrites of the text in which the entrance to Hell is not visible, but none of them worked as well for me as the original version. I was determined to keep things as they were.

This time, the director and the designer came together. And the designer made no allusion to his earlier visit. Nor, I noticed, had he made any change to the illustration of Kierkegaard. That still showed a pencil-slim young dandy with a cane. The director, prompted by common sense and the warnings of long experience, asked about the original production of the play. It's only ego-tripping *young* directors who never want to know what was done before. I told him that for its premiere the play had been done to my complete satisfaction by the young Irish director, Patrick Sandford and that Kierkegaard had been most movingly played by Stephen MacDonald – an excellent English actor who is not a hunchback. The director gave me a startled glance but I was smiling at the designer. The *original* costume designer, I continued, was a talented girl called Janet Scarfe who'd created the effect of sumptuously expensive clothes on a low budget, and still managed to afford a hump for the philosopher.

I asked the director if he'd known Kierkegaard was a hunchback.

'No. But I'm not surprised.' He shrugged. 'God compensates.'

I glanced again at the designer and saw him realise he'd lost the first battle.

But he'd no intention of giving in on the much more important issue of the trap. 'It can't be done,' he declared flatly.

'Why not?' I asked. 'You could build a false stage.' By this I meant a raised platform in which a suitable opening could be cut.

The director bit his lip. 'We'd lose a lot of seating.' In the Vivian Beaumont the seats run right down to practically level with the stage. He repeated in a worried voice, 'Lose seating; else the front row gets a forest of nose hairs.' That is, those nearest the stage would be forced to look directly up at actors – to stare up their noses, in fact.

'Quite unnecessary,' the designer said. 'After all we don't show the entrance to Heaven. Kierkgaard is right there when the play starts.'

'That's because philosophers are more punctual than lechers,' I explained.

'And there's no great relief getting out of Heaven, I suppose,' the director added. I admired the way he was able to compact large areas of discussion into succinct statements.

The argument crackled along for some time between the designer and me and it wasn't clear which of us was making the better case as far as the director was concerned. Finally though, when we paused for breath, he gave his opinion. 'If you're going to do Don Juan – *any* version of Don Juan – you sure as hell better have Hell.'

The designer protested, 'We can have Hell in the wings!'

'That we can't stop,' the director observed tartly. 'But

for the audience, we must have it where they can see it. We must see the *pun*ishment.'

'Absolutely,' I agreed. 'And at the beginning we've got to see him rising from the dead.'

The doorman's buzzer sounded and I went to answer it. He announced, 'Gotta Bernard Cunningham here, wants t'see ya.'

Though feeling that fact and fancy were jostling each other a bit too roughly, I controlled my voice and said, 'Okay. Send him up.' Turning into the room, I apologised. 'I'm sorry about this, but it's someone I must see.'

'Fine,' the director said, rising. 'We're all through for the moment anyway.'

'And I'm all through completely,' the designer said and the angry gurgle in his voice was spoiling for a row. 'There's no way I can go along with nineteenth-century mechanics and a thinking man's Quasi*modo*.'

I smiled at the neatness of the remark but said nothing.

The director sighed and stared at the rug for a few moments, then he said to the designer, 'I think you're right.' But the designer's glitter of triumph was immediately doused. '*You* can't go along with this. So we'll get somebody else to do it.'

The young man snatched up his paraphernalia. He was getting a lot of practice at stormy exits from that apartment. As he threw open the door, Bernard Cunningham was about to press the bell. The director ignored his ex-colleague's tantrum. He told me, 'Come down to the theatre tomorrow afternoon. We'll work it out.' I went with him to the door and invited my next visitor in.

As I'd already noted, Bernard was very much as his discarded clothes had suggested. About six foot, slim hips, heavy shoulders. Generally speaking, a handsome man with brown eyes, American-looking teeth and a sallow complexion. There was one detail, though, which puzzled me. 'What happened to your earring?'

He touched his ear. 'What?'

'I believe you used to wear a chain earring.'

'Who told you that?'

'A soap merchant,' I told him. 'Did you?'

'Yes.' He smiled and shrugged engagingly. 'It was part

of my sea-going image. I'm finished with all that now.'

I invited him to sit down and tried to place his accent. He was not a Londoner but there was no marked indication of where he had grown up unless, perhaps, through a good education in the West Country. He had a very pleasant voice. He said, 'I'm a great admirer of your work, Mr Murray.'

'I'm glad to hear it. What aspect of it suits you best?'

He relaxed on the couch, directly above his own concealed personal effects. 'Well, it's not political, for a start.'

'A good start,' I agreed. 'You're not interested in politics, then.'

'Oh, no! I've had enough of that.'

I looked beyond him to the window where a significant event of the day was about to occur. The sun had found the only narrow chink to the west of the apartment which allowed it to send an acute angled beam into the room. This epiphany lasted no more than fifteen minutes, in good conditions, before the bounty was lost behind the Lincoln Towers.

Bernard glanced over his shoulder to see what was holding my attention. 'What is it?'

I switched back to him. 'What is your main interest?'

He confessed with quiet pride, 'I'm a born-again Christian.'

'Ah! Well, I've nothing against born-again Christians; as long as they don't start killing again.'

He jolted a little straighter on the cushions. 'Kill?'

'Oh, yes. They're famous for it – Christians. Surely you know that?'

'Killing who?'

'People who were *not* Christians. But many of their own as well – if they were the wrong sort.'

He grinned as though I must be joking. 'It's a long time since they did that.'

'Nonesense. They're still doing it. In Britain.' I pulled an ashtray into easier reach and lit a cigarette. 'However, that's not what you came to discuss.'

'No,' he said. 'I wanted to talk about your play.'

'And I wanted to talk about your "death".'

145

He smiled again. 'They're part of the same thing. You've no idea how liberating it was for me when I saw *The Only Street*.'

I nodded a little impatiently. Bernard Cunningham really was a very self-possessed young man; and a great smiler. His smile and his voice had more than a touch of Latter Day Saints on the doorstep. That impregnable rightness delivered with such gentle courtesy is quite infuriating; but I tried not to be too hasty. It was going to be a con after all. He was conning himself. The source of his inspiration – as I'd already guessed – was the play I'd written some years earlier about the jewel-maker in Dublin. I'd taken the title from a poem by Emily Dickinson and had quoted part of it in the programme.

To my embarrassment, Bernard now quoted it right back at me:

'The only One I meet
Is God – the only street,
Existence; this traversed
If other news there be
Or admirabler show
I'll tell it you.'

I sighed. 'Nicely spoken.'

He leaned forward earnestly, forearms resting across his thighs and hands clasped. 'That poem must have made a big impression on you, too.'

'Yes. It's the only occasion I know of where the word "admirabler" is used. So you decided you'd follow Martin's example?'

'*Your* example.'

This startled me. 'I beg your pardon?'

He nodded enthusiastically. 'The whole idea you created in that character was just what I was looking for. And it came at exactly the right time. Even that family you made up seemed to fit my situation. I was … elated!'

'And you were mistaken. I did not create that character. Nor did I "make up" his family.'

The young man looked for a moment as though he might reject this canard out of hand. But I nodded firmly, and he said, 'You mean Martin is *real*?'

'He certainly is.'

My guest gave his head a marvelling shake. 'Well – I certainly was impressed by Martin.'

'No,' I said, 'you didn't see Martin. You were impressed by John Hurt who *played* Martin. And it's difficult *not* to be impressed by Mr Hurt – whatever he plays.' I waited for his response to this but he was stalled on the indigestible gristle of the truth. I went on, 'So, you see, whatever inspired you is a long way from me. And yet *I'm* the one you made next-of-kin.'

'No. That came later. The play was what made me run away to sea in the first place. But my mother, then Tricia found out about that.'

'How did they find out?'

'Well, with the first company I sailed for I filled in their form giving my mother as next-of-kin, and her address. Then they got in touch with her about some formality – so she found out and she told Tricia.'

'What does Tricia know about you at the moment?'

'Only that, with Oregal, *you're* my next-of-kin. She was the one who insisted on seeing your play.'

That would explain the girl calling at my agent's office. When Bernard had failed to show up as he should have at Southampton, Tricia would expect me to have news or, failing that, the personal effects. I asked him, 'How did you find out where I was?'

'Easy. Called the personnel department to find out what was happening. That's when I found out they'd screwed everything up.'

'I'd say you've screw it up quite a bit yourself.'

'Oh no! I've got everything clear now – since the moment I accepted Jesus into my life.'

'That was when you were born again?'

'Right. And to cut off all ties with the past I made it look as though I had drowned.' He smiled up at me. 'And it all started with your play. Going to sea started the real voyage of my life. I've got a lot to thank you for, Mr Murray. For making me see the possibilities and telling me, "The only One I meet is God."'

'No. *That* was Emily Dickinson.'

147

He wasn't really listening. 'Your play changed my life. Before that I was...'

'I don't want to know what you were before that. Nor am I much interested in what you become after *this*.'

To my great relief he stopped smiling. 'What do you mean, Mr Murray?'

'Just tell me why you have come here today.'

'Well ... because things didn't work out the way I planned. With the drowning, I mean.'

'Go on.'

'And I wondered if you'd get in touch with my mother and my girl friend to say that I really was drowned.' He looked at me with sombre earnestness now.

'No. I won't. You can go as far out of reach as you like, but I will not tell them you're dead. In fact when it's tomorrow morning in London I'll call them to say you're just fine.'

He seemed genuinely puzzled at my ill-disguised hostility. 'Why? Why would you do that?'

'Because these are people you are going to need before very long. More than they need you, in my opinion.' A rather grim irony occured to me and I smiled. 'Death isn't a trap-door you can open and shut on a whim. So – I'm willing to grant you parole, but you'll have to wait in line to die.' And it did strike me as odd that Bernard was in the wrong play. Of course he would have no place in *any* play, if only because he was far too gullible and mindlessly callous. But he thought he was walking down *The Only Street* when really he ought to have been facing the dreadful statue which exacts retribution from Don Juan.

He said, 'What about the shipping company?'

'They can go on believing you drowned. It'll make them more careful in future.' I got up. 'Excuse me.' He rose to his feet and I pulled his personal effects cabinet into the open. 'There's just one condition.'

'What's that?'

'Stay away from Bruno Caplow. I intend to let him go on thinking you're dead. He trusted you and nothing would be gained by altering that.'

'He's a good guy, Bruno.'

'That was my impression.' I pulled the polished box

upright. 'Now, take your personal effects. Here's the key. Everything's there except the money. That will cover my expenses.'

Bernard was rather dazed at a turn-around more rapid than any ship-owner could wish. He lifted the box and moved towards the door. I went ahead to open it for him. He paused on the threshold and gave me a keen look. 'You're not the least like the person I thought you were.'

'Really. Well, you're pretty much as I thought you'd be. And not in the least like Martin Doyle.'

'Goodbye, Mr Murray.'

'Goodbye.'

To Die in Copenhagen

Some uppity Dane once said, 'Better to die in Copenhagen than to live in Kiel.' And I can see some virtue in the remark. It is better to do almost anything in Copenhagen than elsewhere; and there's plenty of opportunity. The city has civility, beauty and style. It is also remarkably clean and, for a capital, quiet. It is a city which treats its virtues and its vices with the same adult discretion and does not seem to boast about anything. Kiel, on the other hand, is noisy and garish and boasts that it was once the capital of Schleswig-Holstein. The Danes concede that it was, but point out that Schleswig-Holstein was once Danish territory and anything worth keeping in Kiel is there because they put it there.

When they lost the territory they continued to use it as a convenient entry port to the rest of Europe and began thinking of the place rather as the British thought of Calais – disparaging the new owners but willing to afford them the passing trade. All of this was before the great world wars, of course. As Germany's principal naval port, wars brought a sense of purpose to Kiel and transformed it into a huge iron magnet which attracted industry and people and money. This booming prosperity could not be denied and even though people didn't much enjoy living there they certainly wanted to work there. Meanwhile, the domes and spires of Copenhagen merely turned a shade more green.

My first trip abroad was to the Danish capital and I hesitate to tell you the circumstances because, though relevant, they could form an obstruction to the point of this story. I was already writing stories in the early 1950s but the piece which paid for my passage across the North Sea was not fiction.

While working in a colliery office in Durham I'd written a philosophical paper which relied heavily on the works of Søren Kierkegaard. Only one of the English universities to which I sent it even bothered to reply. And that one wanted to know what were my academic qualifications. Finding I had none, they decided I could not possibly have written what I'd written; and even if I had I'd no right to. So, I tried the Kierkegaard Institute in Copenhagen. They invited me over to read the paper and to discuss its implications. That went well and they invited me to come back and lecture there on what seemed to them a very fresh and practical approach to existential philosophy. To me it seemed an excellent way to get out of the coal mine.

Once in Denmark, my story output increased and I entered one of them for a competition whose most celebrated judge was Karen Blixen. The story won first prize but, more valuably, introduced me to the famous writer. I became one of her many protégés. Curiously, she suggested I ought to be writing plays, not fiction. Then she developed the idea to insist that I should use drama in my work at the Institute. It was plain, she said, that I was obsessed with the conflict of appearance and reality. What better way to demonstrate than to use the medium which depends upon that conflict? This notion of drama as a teaching agent is common enough now but at that time it was daring. Certainly it was daring of her to go over over the heads of those who knew better in order to secure for me the facilities I would need.

So in 1958 I went back to Copenhagen. The Institute occupied a former public library in Nansensgade, but the small studio theatre I'd been assigned was on the other side of the dams, tucked into one of the narrow streets behind the Kristus Kirke. And I'd been found lodgings in a private flat. Every evening as I walked back to my lodgings along the edge of the dam I noticed the same old men; each occupying one of the benches which were strung along the flat top of the dyke. Despite the fine weather, they all wore long coats and felt hats. They

151

formed a still-life arrangement in shades of brown and, illuminated by the misty sunset, each one of them looked as though he was posing for Whistler's *Father* or, failing that, a bit-part in a *nocturne*. The music in the air that late summer was the song 'Bonjour Tristesse', which seemed marvellously apt for the patient melancholy of the silent men staring across the stretch of water.

On one bench, though, there were *two* old men. They sat at extreme ends of the bench, presumably to discourage anyone else from sharing it with them, and conducted their conversation across the gap. To my surprise, they spoke with strong Glasgow accents. As I passed, I tried to make out what they were saying, but the Clydeside dialect is at once the most ugly and impenetrable variation on the English language and always sounds as though an argument is in progress. As I walked on, the situation intrigued me. These men who looked like tramps could not be tourists. Their age and the fact of their timeless leisure meant they were not guest-workers. What on earth were they doing in Copenhagen? The Pinteresque quality of their existence prompted me to pose the problem to my students the following day.

Later in the week, at the same spot, an argument certainly *was* in progress. The men were loudly disputing something in a newspaper which was spread out on the bench between them. This time I didn't walk by. Under the pretence that I wanted to have a better look at something across the dam, I clambered up on top of the dyke. The angry voices behind me continued and, turning to resume my walk, I got a good look at the men. One was red-faced and heavy-shouldered, the other was much thinner. Both had false teeth. As I paused, the more dominant man snatched up the paper and smoothed it against his knee. It was a copy of the *Glasgow Herald*. Another surprise. This was much further up-market than I'd given them credit for, and more expensive. Most of the main British newspapers were on sale in the city on the afternoon of their publication, but they were highly-priced special editions printed on flimsy paper. Neither of the men looked as though he could afford such a luxury.

When I got to the digs my mail was laid out on a table in

the heavily waxed hallway. And there was a copy of my local weekly newspaper. Immediately, I thought of the men on the dyke. If they wanted to keep in touch with what was happening at home, why didn't *they* have their friends or family send them the local news? My reflection was interrupted by my landlady returning from her work at the hospital. She bade me good-day and, as she let herself into her living room, mimed complete exhaustion and her intention to flake out that very moment. Mime was the usual means of communication between my landlady and myself. I could not speak Danish and she could not speak English. In this she was an exception, for Copenhagen is a bilingual city. Practically everyone you meet in the streets or in shops or in offices can speak English very well indeed. That Fru Rasmussen could not was a matter of class, not ignorance. Her family had been landed gentry and in her generation it was accepted that one only learned English if one intended to sell something *to* the English. In short, it was a trade language.

She'd married a wealthy businessman, but he had died bankrupt just after the war. He left her very poorly off and all she had was crammed into this old flat. Even so, she probably would not have taken in a lodger if she'd not known him to be a friend of the Baroness Blixen-Finecke. She thought of me as a guest rather than a lodger and I solved the awkwardly recurring subject of money by sending her a cheque by post each month, to the value of D.kr.400. It seemed a slight enough gesture of respect for a woman who was once a leader of Copenhagen society, with a fine seat to horse, horses, and servants to light the candles for dinner.

The puzzle of the combative Scotsmen would soon have gone out of mind had it not been for a rather tiresome idiosyncracy of my own. Again I hesitate to be specific because of the irritation it may cause. And whereas detailing my involvement at the Kierkegaard Institute is likely to offend only those who believe that young coal miners shouldn't be able to think – much less write – the next aberration cannot help but offend a much larger section of the public – those who enjoy food. Neverthe-less, it is a fact that from an age when I was able to have

153

some say in the matter *I've* been offended by people eating and have sought to spare them the offence of watching me do it. People eating in public disgusts me as much as people excreting in public might disgust others. Fortunately, there was at least one restaurant on Copenhagen where I could eat out. It was at the equivalent of a Salvation Army hostel. The Lutheran authorities had discovered that property-damaging fights were most likely to break out between their charges at meal times. Consequently, they had constructed the dining area around three sides of the large, rectangular kitchen. The serving surface was divided into individual cubicles, much in the fashion of snugs in some old English public houses. It was there I went for my main meal of the day.

One evening I heard familiar voices, and this time I could make out what they were saying because they were calling through adjoining cubicles to each other. The Scotsmen were disputing where the German battle-cruiser *Gneisenau* had been built and launched. The softer voice claimed it for Kiel. It stood to reason since both Gneisenau and Scharnhorst had been Prussian generals against Napoleon. My eyes widened. I had not known that. The loud voice overruled him, displaying a close knowledge of the strength and personnel of the Kriegsmarine. As a clincher he asserted that he knew a man who'd built *Gneisenau* and saw Hitler launch her at Blohm and Voss in Hamburg.

I was astonished by the excellent German pronunciation of these names and of several jaw-breaking compounds of competing shipyards and admirals alluded to in passing. It occurred to me that probably both men spoke German better than they spoke English. And they spoke Danish, too, for there were several asides to the food servers, delivered in easy colloquial manner.

All this made nonsense of the little improvisations I'd conducted with my students in which the Scotsmen were cast as ignorant yobbos who'd merely found a copy of the *Glasgow Herald* and could barely read it. In the funny little scene we'd worked out, the newspaper was coveted because the size and number of its pages provided excellent insulation when worn around the body. With faith in my own perception somewhat shaken, I decided I ought to meet my fellow diners. When I'd finished my meal I waited in the long, antiseptic-smelling corridor for the Scotsmen to appear. They took a long time over their evening meal and while I waited my assurance dwindled. There was absolutely no reason why they should satisfy my curiosity. They hadn't asked to be used as lay figures in a private demonstration. Why should they give a damn that it had proved false? Obviously, I'd better invent an excuse for talking to them. But when they came strolling down the corridor I still had not thought of anything convincing.

They looked younger without their hats and overcoats. In a warm building after a good meal they even managed some jauntiness. And they were not the same age. The big man certainly was no more than sixty and the shorter, thinner man probably in his mid-fifties. Both of them seemed perfectly at ease as they chatted amiably together. The big man noticed me and I could see he was trying to place where he'd seen me before. I still hadn't thought of a good excuse and they walked past me. But they did not walk far. The big man suddenly stopped, then strode back towards me in a purposeful way. Even before he reached me he started talking in rapid, glottal Danish. I stared at him, quite mystified. But of course he would assume I was Danish. Whatever he was saying his companion felt it either unneccesary or offensive. He remained standing far down the corridor and several times called on 'Allan' to forget it. But Allan had no intention of forgetting it and when he'd finished his pitch waited for me to respond. In my confusion I did not reply in English but instead blurted out one of my three Danish phrases. I asked him if *he* could speak English. And, as it happened, that was the best thing to do. After a brief stunned pause, he burst out laughing.

His name was Allan Chalmers. He was born in Clydebank in 1898, left school at fourteen, immediately went to work in the shipyards and gradually gained promotion from tea-boy to labourer to 'hauder-on' to hole-borer to rivetter. I'd had no idea the business of fastening one steel plate to another could be so labour-intensive.

Allan's companion had enjoyed a much quieter life. His name was Donal McLaverty and he wasn't a Scotsman at all. He was from Cork originally, but as a young man emigrated to Clydeside in search of a job. As a precision driller, he was used to much more delicate work than Allan and had been employed on the engineering side. However, when that failed he stabbed his pride and deserted the dry, clean engine shops to take his chances outside, perched high and soaked on the frozen rusty side of a vast hulk as a hole-borer. I foolishly remarked that hole-boring and drilling were the same thing. Both men gave me a pitying look.

All this information was easily extracted in our first conversation right there in the supervised common room of the hostel. My interest in their work interested them and they did not mind that my pursuit of it was entirely selfish. While they talked I kept building up little pictures of novel mimes which I could set my students. Since the business of rivetting demands so much physical co-ordination and co-operation the subject was ideal.

And the men were very good at sharing a conversation. Of course, most men are better at sharing a conversation than women but the Allan/Donal method was particularly engaging. They enjoyed each other's company and wanted me to enjoy the best of their stories. They prompted each other to recall amusing anecdotes and, though both of them knew all of them by heart, whichever of them was listening listened as though he hadn't heard it before. It was not until I was on my feet and ready to leave that I asked why they were in Copenhagen. Without consulting one another by word or movement of the head, they each returned suddenly frozen and hostile stares. The response was puzzling but, since there was no use to which I could put the answer in any case, it didn't bother me. I just nodded, bade them goodbye and smuggled out a haul of illustrated fragments under the illusion that I had captured the whole reality of two lives.

Apart from subject matter for my work, the meeting with Allan Chalmers and Donal McLaverty sharpened my awareness of Copenhagen. Before I met them, my idea of the city was confined to its centre. I'd taken delight in the broad tree-lined streets, the open squares with their parquet flooring of bricks and, always upon some vista, a fairy-tale palace rising from its grassy moat. At every corner, too, there seemed to be the smell of cigar smoke and freshly ground coffee. Most pervasive of all, though, was the sound of bells. There seemed to be bells of every size and pitch being gently played. Churches had them, clocks had them, shops, roundsmen, and tradesmen had them. Students wore them and there were thousands of cyclists who had and used them.

Nearly as pervasive were the glimpses of water. But somehow I did not connect the dams, the river and the canals with the sea, until I heard Allan Chalmers refer to it with such relish. For Copenhagen is one of the few capital cities which is actually on the seashore. It is stretched along a finger of the Baltic which pokes up into the Kattegat. In the misty autumn weather that year I often went down to the waterfront, where the air is so salty you can practically feel the grains rattling up your nose when you breathe in. There the insistent bells are left behind or overcome by the horns and sirens of ships which are all on 'slow-ahead' and wary. Many of them were still using steam horns which, in a way, made sound visible. You see a white plume suddenly appear on the side of the funnel and after a few moments the note of the plume reaches you.

Apart from the activity at sea the place was bustling, for København is a market harbour and its market-stall is packed with goods a mile or so wide and about forty miles long. There were also docks and ship repair yards. I wondered if Donal and Allan had worked there. Perhaps they became redundant when the practice of rivetting stopped. That would be during the war. Indeed, I recalled Allan pointing out that if you're really serious about destruction there's no time to waste on rivetting. Four men were soon replaced by one incandescent, hooded welder.

In the flat, Fru Rasmussen and I continued to give spirited performances even when describing to each other the vagaries of the weather. She was a short, rather plump, cheerful woman and the web of wrinkles at her eyes showed she had laughed a great deal. On first meeting her my impression was of a very merry widow in her mid-forties. But shortly afterwards there was a national census. When she gave me the partly completed form so that my own details could be added, I was amazed to discover she was sixty-three. And, apparently, she didn't care who knew it – otherwise she could have had me make my entry before she made hers.

Despite that, and though she did not go out very much, she led a very active home life which often encroached upon the fabric of my digs. It was a very old flat and in constant need of repair. When, for example, the bathroom window needed reglazing, she entertained a very practical young man for the night. I know how young he was because he mistakenly burst into *my* room when the hilarity was at its pitch. When I returned the following evening the same young man was putting the finishing touches to a new bathroom window.

She also knew – or knew where she could find – carpenters and painters. Everyone involved seemed to be very happy about the system and I was ready to conclude that my hostess had the ease, confidence and charm to make the whole business of sex fresh and sweet and great fun. But she did not waste her time. Unfortunately, there was no aspect of her life which required the talents of a writer or theatre director. On one occasion, though, she did engage me as a witness.

It happened on a very quiet evening. I was in my room working on a lecture and lulled by the hum of my electric typewriter. Very distantly – because the doors fitted so well – I could hear the sound of laughter on Fru Rasmussen's television set. Earlier, she had invited me in to watch one of the many English programmes with Danish subtitles. Then came an almighty, splitting, fracturing and attenuated crash. The surprise and sheer volume of the noise bolted me to my chair for several moments then I threw open the door to see my hostess in a posture of abject despair leaning against the entrance to the kitchen and staring down. The floor of the kitchen was about four inches thick in broken dishes, crockery, china and glassware. Moreover, access to the stove was blocked by the huge wood cabinet which had held them, running the full length of the wall. It had dropped off and was now wedged, upended and splintered between the sink unit and the stove. When I'd taken in the awesome extent of this devastation, Fru Rasmussen indicated that she was offering me some coffee. I thanked her but signalled my willingness to help her clear up the mess – or at least hack a path through it. She shook her head reprovingly. That, apparently, would have spoiled the whole object of the exercise. It had to be left exactly as it was until the insurance man came the following day. And that meant the stove couldn't be used until then. With that likelihood in mind, Fru Rasmussen had made coffee *before* the blitz and I cheerfully accepted it.

The insurance man was still there when I got back from the studio next day. Switching to English, he asked me if I'd been home when the accident happened. I told him I was. In fact, Fru Rasmussen and I had been watching television together in her living-room when disaster struck in the kitchen. I saw a gleam of appreciation in the eyes of my hostess – which sorted ill with the mask of tragedy she was doing her best to maintain.

For, of course, it was a tragic loss. Fru Rasmussen's heirlooms and treasures collected over a lifetime, objects of sentimental value and objects of even greater monetary value had all been destroyed. The only positive aspect of the whole affair was that, not more than a week earlier, Fru Rasmussen had occasion to 'tidy' the enormous cabinet. It was a great help to the claims inspector that she was able to tell him exactly what had been lost. While she related the details she made little darting swoops to pluck up this jagged fragment, or a shard of that. Getting into the swing of it, she finally disinterred an almost whole teapot and stood there recalling its history; for all the world like Hamlet, fondling a larger than usual skull of Yorick. Whether or not the insurance man was taken in it was difficult to say but she got the money she needed for a trip to Italy. Apparently her very old, and still wealthy, mother-in-law lived there. Fru Rasmussen had no intention of letting neglect of the fact exclude her from any suitable provisions in the old lady's will.

After my first proper meeting with the men from Clydebank I found it oddly difficult to meet them again. Though I was quite familiar with their routine, it no longer seemed to coincide with mine. Even when I did spot them at the hostel, or in the streets nearby, they always had something to do which precluded any idle chit-chat. Yet I knew perfectly well they had nothing to do and how they tried to stretch every minor activity in an effort to fill the empty days. I was somewhat affronted to realise that they were avoiding me. Since it did not occur to me that I was other than a wholly engaging and sympathetic person, the fault must be theirs.

What, I wondered, were they hiding? Was there some crime they'd committed? My thoughts first turned to burglary or robbery. It could be, I supposed, that when they'd been laid off during the Depression they had turned to illegal means for making money. Maybe they'd robbed a bank and were still wanted by the police in Scotland. Or maybe it was worse than that. Considering the time which had elapsed, only murder seemed serious enough to keep them in hiding still.

As it turned out, I was wrong about the nature of their crime though right about its gravity. But the facts would not have come to me at all if the men had not abruptly fallen out with each other. Whatever caused the row, the consequences were immediately obvious. Each man was plainly on his own. They occupied well-separated cubicles for meals, and if Donal was in the common room when Allan got there, he just turned and walked back down the corridor. Strangely, though, neither of them took up with new friends. Probably they'd never imagined the necessity might arise and so had quite forgotten how it was done. Or, just as likely, the other men in the hostel wanted nothing to do with the strangers – either as a pair or singly.

At about the same time as Fru Rasmussen staged armageddon in the kitchen, Donal McLaverty was planning a trip as well. And, since he had no family heirlooms to destroy, he decided to cadge the money from the only person of his acquaintance who seemed to have ready cash. That was me.

Donal came to see me at the studio. He interrupted right at the start of an afternoon session and said he wanted to talk to me. I suggested he might like to sit at the back of the tiny auditorium until I'd finished my lecture. Since it was warm and comfortable he readily agreed. And he listened to the lecture with great interest, leaning over the seat in front of him. And at the end he asked questions. To illustrate his points, he made detailed reference to the plays of Bernard Shaw. He'd never actually seen any of the plays in a theatre – which seemed to me a wise precaution – but he'd read the least boring of them several times. All this was of no interest to my students. For their generation, and mine, Shaw never wrote anything for the stage which would not have been more apt and less irritating in a dilettante socialist weekly.

When the students had gone, Donal came to the point. Above all, he wanted to go home to Ireland. It was his opinion that things were looking up there and, at fifty-five, he still had a chance of getting a job. I regarded him intently. We sat in the front row of seats and even with the flattery of stage lighting the man did not look fit enough for work. He was thin and his awkward, angular movements strengthened that impression. He had a sharp, foxy face with deep-set eyes and heavy brows, but it was the pallor of his skin which made me doubt if he was in good health.

I'd guessed as soon as he appeared at the door that Donal was going to ask me for money and I'd no intention of giving him any. However, he didn't know that and now that I held him as a sort of hostage it seemed a good opportunity to extort the facts which had been denied me before. He seemed willing to pay the price. Free of Allan Chalmers' dominating presence, the thin Irishman with the Scottish accent started his recital there in the theatre. He continued when we went out on the street where an early flurry of snow was blowing. Since we'd overshot the time when meals were available at the hostel I took him

161

back to the flat for something to eat. He told a curious yet inevitable story.

In the early 1930s both Donal and Allan were working at Clydebank and were laid off at the same time. Allan lived with his mother and two sisters while Donal lodged with another family in the town. For a while he courted Norma, the younger of the Chalmers sisters, but she married someone who'd managed to hold on to a job even when the effects of the economic depression were most keen. It was that rejection as much as Allan's enterprising spirit which made him agree the time had come to leave Scotland and search for work elsewhere. Now that the newly married couple had moved in with the Chalmers, Allan felt free to use his dole money entirely on his own behalf and moved out to share Donal's room in digs. But it was still the same town and still the same hopeless lack of work. Nor were there even the slightest indications that things might improve. In Allan's opinion there was nothing for it but to look further afield. Now there was some security in his family's home, his enterprising nature dictated some positive effort and he easily persuaded his friend to go along.

Donal and Allan hitch-hiked down as far as the midlands but the situation was no better there. In fact it was worse. They were treated as pernicious job-snatchers and told to keep walking. Donal was used to being treated as an undesirable alien by the English but Allan took it very hard. He'd never been in England before. And now even the lorry drivers who stopped to give them a lift had only to hear their accents to slam the cab door shut in their faces and drive on without them.

The aliens kept walking. The physical effort was not a great hardship for the young men and their anger served only to increase their energy. It was summer, and if nothing else turned up they could always join the army of fruit-pickers in Kent – even if they had to pretend they were deaf and dumb to avoid discrimination. But it didn't come to that. When they reached London's dockland they heard talk of a remarkable opportunity. Some shipyard abroad was looking for skilled men. The money was good and the only condition was that applicants should be under thirty, healthy and with no dependants. Donal and Allan joined the line and were briskly interviewed by a German manager who had no idea which accents were acceptable in England. He did know what he needed, though, and hired the men. A few days later they went ashore in Kiel.

During a very brief settling-in period they soon learned the open secret of Germany's contravention of the Versailles treaty. In order to evade treaty obligations and the rather flaccid operation of the control commission, the recently empowered Nazis did not at first build complete submarines in one place. Various parts were fabricated all over Germany so that the steel requirements and machinery orders were never separately large enough to arouse suspicion. But these parts were then collected at Kiel and assembled in some secrecy.

Donal and Allan were recruited in the squad assembling U-boats. That required a lot of rivetting. The men from Clydebank tackled their work with vigour. They were quite overcome by the transition from sad, despairing dole queues to a bustling, affluent boom town. For the first time in their lives they had more money than they needed to live comfortably and it produced a heady feeling of freedom. The only limitation was that they were not allowed to send money home to their respective families. All the recruits had asserted their lack of dependants in order to get a job, and now they were held to it.

Of course, there was no question yet of any strained relations between Britain and Germany. Herr Hitler was still being lauded in the English press for the economic miracle he was achieving. Unemployment was falling at an amazing rate in the Third Reich. Steel production roared ahead and all the shipyards were busy. So, while all that could be offered on the Clyde was a tentative suggestion to resume work on the abandoned, rusting hulk of No.534, on the Elbe the beautiful lines of *Scharnhorst* and *Gneisenau* were already rising from the slipways.

The guest workers and native workers alike took great pride in what they were doing. Gradually, the guests began to identify with their hosts. There were night classes in German language, literature and culture. Skill and ability were recognised and rewarded. Donal married a German girl and settled on the outskirts of Kiel. Allan kept his independence, and added to it when he rented a flat in one of the new blocks which were sprouting on the headland overlooking the Kleine Bucht.

Whereas English literature had passed him by when his whole attention was taken up with mere survival, Allan avidly pursued Goethe, Heine and Thomas Mann now that he had a full stomach and no fear of eviction. At work, his ease of learning and natural ability earned him promotion. By the time the Nazis abandoned all subterfuge and set about a full building programme, Allan Chalmers was a foreman.

And it was then his doubts began. Obviously, such an armada of warships under construction at Kiel and in other yards must have some purpose. The argument of self-defence began to ring hollow when it became apparent that none of the European neighbours was making even threatening noises. In fact, the only noise they were making was 'tut, tut'.

If he'd not been educated in Germany, Allan would never have given politics a second thought. The subject had held no interest for him at home. In his estimation the Red Clydesiders had been no more than a bunch of cranky self-publicists; and he'd wished to God that Jimmie Maxton would get his *hair* cut. He'd formed a similarly dismissive opinion about the gung-ho Englishmen who were trooping into Spain to fight against Franco. His own memory of fighting the gauleiters of the English for food obscured any virtue there might be in their fighting for a cause. Certainly there would be damn few Scotsmen waving their arms in Spain. From his point of view the unfortunate thing was that if England went to war with Germany she'd drag Scotland in with her.

Donal McLaverty was in an easier position. When war came, *his* country was not dragged in. Ireland declared neutrality. He could go on working happily enough for a friendly power. But not long after the outbreak of war his wife died with a stillborn child. Suddenly, there was nothing to hold him in Germany. He gave up his house and, for company if nothing else, went to share the flat with Allan Chalmers. It began to seem as though they were irrevocably tied to each other. At home or abroad, destitute or well-paid, they always came back to depending on each other. Together they now considered the future. In particular *their* future if Germany lost the war. Whereas they had few scruples about profiting as collaborators they had no intention of being punished for it. They decided they would escape from Germany and return to the most virtuous nation on earth, while its virtue was still intact and their sins might be forgiven them.

The escape route could not have been simpler. Shipyard craftsmen were often required to sail with a newly commissioned boat to carry out last minutes adjustments or to correct faults which only appeared when the vessel was handed over to the navy. In peacetime there would be proper trials but at the breakneck pace of the Kriegsmarine the first voyage was the trial, and the slow progress along the seventy miles of the Kiel canal was the only testing area available.

Normally the test squad went ashore before the canal reached the Elbe estuary and were transported by rail back to Kiel. When Donal and Allan got ashore they planned to go into hiding and then make their way on foot down the north bank of the estuary and get aboard a neutral freighter when she stopped to let the river pilot off. They did get to the estuary all right, but the date was 15 March 1941 and the newspapers were celebrating a great blow which had been struck by the Luftwaffe. On the two previous nights Clydebank had been blitzed into ruins.

There was no question now of Allan going home. According to the papers there was no home to go back to and it seemed unlikely that any of his family had survived. The two men got back on the train for Kiel. Neither of them said a word to the other for the whole of the tedious journey, but each understood perfectly well that they were finished building U-boats.

In the days that followed they devised a new plan. If they could get into occupied Denmark there was a possiblity of escaping across the narrow strait to neutral Sweden. The Nazi traffic was moving the other way, with

Danish Jews and other workers wanted elsewhere in the Reich arriving in boatloads at Kiel harbour. But the boats went back empty. That is how Donal and Allan reached Copenhagen. They smuggled themselves aboard an empty floating tumbril. But the Resistance men laughed at the very idea of granting them precious places in the escape line. They were traitors, and whereas the Danes would not shop them to the Nazis, they'd better keep out of everybody's way if they wanted to stay alive. Allan pleaded to be allowed to put his case to the Baroness in person but was told she would whip him where he stood.

'The Baroness.' As soon as Donal said that, my attention veered wildly away from the story he was telling. 'The Baroness' was Karen Blixen, of course. For a moment the blanched skeleton of her living face and the enormous dark eyes stared into my mind and I felt certain that – in another sphere, perhaps – this random meeting had been arranged. The only reason I was in Copenhagen was because of her and the only reason Donal had not been able to leave it was because of her.

The story he had told up to that point was unsatisfactory because it was no more than a recital of facts. It reported an outer world of reality which I was too young to know much about. And, in any case, I placed more reliance on an inner world of literature and philosophy. That inner world – though rich and fraught and packed with variety – was insulated against many things. Chiefly, I now realised, it was insulated against Time. And, in literature, coincidence always has a purpose. It was unsettling to hear that in the outer world coincidence is common and pointless and conclusive. If, for example, the men had chosen a different week to escape from Kiel and had arrived at the Elbe estuary on any other day than the one on which the Clydebank blitz was announced – they would have escaped. They would not now be traitors and exiles. And I would not now be concerned. But I'd sat in the sunlit morning room at Rungstedlund and listened to Karen Blixen tell of the hair's-breadth escapes in which she'd been involved; about the brave and reckless people she'd hidden in the house, waiting for the best opportunity to smuggle them across the Sound into Sweden.

166

Literary coincidence would dictate that, if anyone, I should meet one of those grateful refugees. The coincidence of reality dictated that I should meet a traitor and willing collaborator with the Nazis.

Yet I still held to the artistic verity that there is no coincidence without purpose – whether it is perversely real or not. As Donal's voice went on it seemed I was not listening, but merely storing the information for later. Uppermost was the certainty that I was there to provide the escape the Baroness had refused to consider. What made the great difference was Time. The men who had found their path so effectively blocked were too old now to be traitors. Quite arbitrarily the world had said forgive and forget – forgetting that, unlike nations, men cannot often forgive themselves. Europe had healed and they were no more than microscopic callouses on a healthy skin. And the vigorous passionate woman who'd defended the gate to freedom was very old too. Up at Rungstedlund, reduced to a very whisper of femininity, Karen Blixen was dying.

Now Donal was telling me he wanted to go home. Allan had done all he could to dissuade him. That had been the cause of their argument and estrangement. The senior man asserted that it didn't make any difference being Irish if you were a traitor to England. Lord Haw-Haw was Irish but the English hanged him just the same. Donal reported this as a rueful joke but I could see he'd been affected by it. I did my best to reassure him. What was more – while still subject to the powerful influence of poetic justice if not moral justice – I changed my mind and promised I would help in his last escape bid. But it would have been foolish to give him the money for his fare. Instead, I offered to book and pay for his passage by rail to Esbjerg and by sea to Cork. When, finally, he left the flat he was a happy man.

My reflection on the disorderly past would have been even more unsettling if I'd known of a further coincidence which was to emerge before long, and which put me squarely in the camp of the traitors. But next morning the immediate preoccupation was with Allan Chalmers. I saw him waiting for me across the road as soon as I emerged

167

from the flat's entrance. His long coat looked bulkier than ever and between the severely tilted cap and the coils of a scarf his face was very red. He lurched onto the roadway and made a threatening line straight at me. I waited. There were no preliminaries. He was taller than I and stood very close as he delivered an angry denunciation of me, my conduct and McLaverty, who was nothing but a sponger and a weasel for bringing me into it at all. I should, he told me, learn to mind my own business and not behave like a typical Englishman (never to be trusted anyway) who thought he had a God-given right to play the bloody squire of the manor *wherever* he happened to be. There was, as well, the fact that letting McLaverty loose wouldn't help him in the least. What was there for him in Ireland? It would break the bastard's heart when he found out there was nobody wanted him. As for getting work over there, he hadn't the chance of a snowball in hell of holding a job in his condition. Finally, he supposed I knew that I'd never get my money back. I didn't have a *cat* in hell's chance of that.

To all of this I made no reply, though I did note the odd gestures he made to emphasise the points he made. They were curiously out of sync. with the voice. Later, this nagged at my attention until I realised that the gestures were *not* meant to emphasise the words in a way that an actor would co-ordinate them. The sweeping, emphatic gestures and the movements of head and body were a complete and separate statement. They were the outward signs of a frantic man drowning. There was nothing I could do about that. If Donal stayed with him they would both drown. When the big man stumped away from me it was as much as he could do to keep that arrogant, upright posture.

Donal told me that Allan was against his leaving Copenhagen but either did not know or did not care why that should be so. They had been friends for a long time, of course; thirty years. But the parting of old friends was nowhere near the crux. They were each other's sole support, justification and argument for the existence they'd pursued for so long. Each was to the other the only link with home – though a link which had been detached

168

from the rest of the chain. Surely a link was the irreducible minimum which could still be identified as part of a chain? Yet Donal wanted to split even that fragment apart. It was difficult to see why he should want to do so, *now*. The explanation he'd given me was less than convincing, and obviously Allan didn't believe it, either. He'd said he wanted to get work in Ireland so that he could get into the system and prove himself eligible for a retirement pension when the time came. Repeatedly he'd pointed out that he was five years younger than Allan Chalmers. He was sure he could still get work; no matter what it might be, he wasn't fussy. And he did not want to die in Copenhagen. That was nearer the mark. He knew he was ill; perhaps failing rapidly. Allan knew it too and resented it. His friend's illness weakened them both if it drove one of them home.

By the end of that week I'd made the arrangements and Donal came to the flat to collect his tickets. As far as officialdom knew, here was a Danish citizen visiting friends in Ireland for Christmas. I saw him off on the first leg of the journey. Allan wasn't there and the eager traveller made no reference to the man who had governed his life in exile. Instead, he was anxious to convince me that the money I'd spent on him would be repaid. Several times he patted the inside pocket of his coat to establish that he had my address in a safe place. Once he actually took the postcard out of the pocket and had me examine what he'd written, as though the street and the number and the district were in themselves a surety of his inflexible purpose.

When the boat-train started off with a shower of accelerating sparks I was heartily glad that such a tedious formality was over. I hurried out of the side entrance of the station and, for a moment, was certain that I saw the lumbering figure of Allan Chalmers crossing towards the high, locked gates of the Tivoli Gardens. The figure was immediately obscured by traffic but, quite irrationally, I felt reassured. It was as though by his presence Allan, however reluctantly, had conferred a blessing. He would give no spoken credence to this desertion; but how could he resist watching the moment when the link was broken? I smiled and to myself quoted:

169

'Kindred and long companionship, withal,
Most high Athena, are things magical'

My classes were suspended for the Christmas break and I had planned to have a short holiday in England, but Fru Rasmussen had not yet returned from Italy and I felt I shouldn't leave the flat unguarded. The change of plans also enabled me to get some writing done instead of spending unproductive time visiting friends and family.

My feelings of remorse grew stronger. It was clear that in helping one man I'd done a great disservice to the other. And I could think of no way in which I might be of use to Allan Chalmers. But the feeling of guilt persisted so, during that Christmas break, I spent a lot of time at the hostel. At first he didn't want to talk to me. Then he only wanted to harangue me and castigate the English. Finally – when he'd run out of breath, as it were – he was willing to declare a truce.

It was then he discovered I was not accusing him of anything; not even covertly. There was no resentment on my part that he seemed to detest the English. Any Englishman who lives abroad and stays away from embassies must soon come to terms with the fact that half the world detests the English. Nor could I bring myself to feel any moral indignation about his treachery. Considerations of that sort were simply not my business. If it had been my business, though, I would have done the same thing he did.

What Allan Chalmers and I had in common was that we were working-class and therefore not concerned with soul-searching about the rights and futilities of war. He and I both knew that it is only middle-class people who can stop wars because it is middle-class people who start them. The urge to conquer other lands is merely a progression of the inbred desire to own property. Neither of us had ever owned or had the slightest desire to own property. It was curious, therefore, that he felt himself to be a traitor merely because he'd worked for the enemies of a neighbouring country. That is the sort of idealism which only property owners can afford. Allan quite saw my point and dismissed it. What lay at the root of his malaise

170

was the fact that he'd worked for the state which had killed his entire family and their friends.

He'd written home as soon as the war was over. The original letter and its envelope were returned to him under official cover. He showed me the documents. On the envelope he'd posted to the Dalmuir district of Clydebank there was the broad imprint of a rubber stamp which brusquely stated, 'CONDEMNED'. Apparently the post office was using the nearest appropriate pre-war stamps for undelivered mail but the single word conveyed a rather eerie accusation in itself.

The letter had then been passed on to the Relocation Office at the town hall and a printed 'Bomb Damage' slip was inserted which listed all the council property in that area which had been demolished. His home was on the list. There was no mention of the people who'd once lived there. The post office and the Relocation Office, too, were solely concerned with property. Allan then wrote to the nearest address which wasn't on the list. The tenant immediately wrote back to confirm that none of the Chalmers family had survived.

So – there was no going back because there was nothing to go back to; and those who had come through the blitz would know why *he* was alive. At first Allan was overcome with sorrow and shame, but as the personal grief lessened he built up defences to cope with the terrible despair at his own life. He grew resentful of the country which had forced him abroad to look for work. Bolstered by the faithful support of Donal McLaverty, he grew bitter and assertive. This crystallised over the years into an almost constant state of frustrated anger. He blustered and shouted, as I knew, but that was all show. His gestures and unconsidered movements betrayed a man who knew he had betrayed himself; and would never forgive.

And now there was no one to impress with the show and no one whose mere presence confirmed they'd been right to do what they did. Donal had surrendered just when another, more potent, enemy was gaining ground. That enemy, of course, was Time. Allan was sixty and felt he could no longer sustain the image he had presented for so long. Yet he had nothing with which to replace it. The bulk was gnawed away from inside and the shell would soon collapse.

When he got to the stage of admitting this to me, a couple of weeks had elapsed and we were in the flat. Getting him to accept my invitation had been as difficult to achieve as getting him to tell me the truth. But there he was; resting comfortably in my armchair and drinking the beer I'd provided. It was a measure of his wretchedness that he was asking a man of my age and nationality what he should do. It was my opinion that he had what Kierkegaard calls 'the sickness unto death', but it would have been less than friendly to tell him so. As to a course of action – being the man he was and with no practice in being any other – there was nothing he could do but wait. What I told him, though, was more heartening and practical. I suggested he should go back to live in Kiel. He laughed and nodded his head admiringly. That had never occurred to him but it was an entirely sensible idea. He spoke excellent German, he got on with the people, and there he would not be an outcast. But I knew he wouldn't do it.

We were interrupted by Fru Rasmussen who, very kindly – and no doubt to satisfy her curiosity – had made coffee for us and prepared some pastry. I helped her with the tray and Allan got to his feet. After the introductions she was delighted to find what she called an 'Englishman' who could speak Danish – and speak it so well. For a while she rattled away nineteen to the dozen, catching up with all the things she'd wanted to tell me. My guest was pressed into service as interpreter. Thus we both learned that her mother-in-law was *still* hale and hearty and Fru Rasmussen was able to assure her that she had not remarried. This last remark was clarified much later to the effect that Fru Rasmussen's main hope of the old lady's will would be blighted if she stopped being the sorrowing widow of the old lady's son. Soon, Allan gave up translating and they chatted for a while in lively fashion while I was left sustaining a fixed smile to cover my annoyance at the intrusion.

My work at the studio had resumed after the holiday

and again I took up the routine of going to the hostel for my evening meal. On most occasions I saw Allan in the common room afterwards, and one evening I was very happy to report that Donal *had* returned the money I'd spent on his passage home. There was no letter or news of how he was faring – just the money in punt notes. Allan was not impressed and made it plain his old friend was relegated to non-person by his desertion. In any case the shifty bastard had probably stolen the money.

Of much greater importance to me was another letter I received about the same time. It was from Karen Blixen. She invited me to visit her because she would be going into a Copenhagen hospital soon and could be there for some time. It was plain that she guessed what I knew; that her stay in hospital would be brief and she would die there. Next morning I made an appearance at the studio to cancel the day's session, then set out northwards for Rungstedlund in a vulnerable condition of angry sadness.

It was a wasted journey. At the house Clara Svendsen stood guard. She was Karen Blixen's companion and secretary who now, after sixteen years at the task, had absolute authority over who should and who should not see the Baroness. From the moment she saw me crossing the little rustic bridge she'd made up her mind that I should not. In vain did I flourish the invitation I'd received. Clara told me the Baroness was in no condition to see anyone. Surely I must realise her patient was an old woman and very sick. My impetuous protest was that I'd received a letter from Scheherazade and I'd not be put off by a sick old woman.

Clara stared at me impassively but did not budge an inch from her upright stance in the hall made bright by the afternoon sunlight. She would tell the Baroness that I'd called. She would have offered me some coffee but there was such a great deal for her to do in preparing to move her patient into hospital. Perhaps I would visit there, when I was permitted. For the moment, there was nothing more to say. And so I left the house thinking I'd never have another occasion to go back there.

As I waited for the Copenhagen train in a freezing wind the thought occurred to me that I should write another story for Karen Blixen. I'd tell her a tale of the men from the Clyde who helped build the U-boats of Kiel. Particularly I would stress her part in their exile. As the train moved slowly down the coast, the idea strengthened. There were many ironies in the situation which would appeal to her if she had the time to read it. I glanced out as we approached the northern suburbs of the city at Klampenborg. In front of every villa or cottage there was a flagpole and on every pole the national flag strained and snapped in the constant wind of Denmark. That day was not a special occasion. The ordinary householders raised and lowered their flag every day.

When I got back to the flat it seemed a good omen that Allan Chalmers was waiting for me there; or so I thought at the time. Fru Rasmussen had let him wait in my room since she knew him to be a friend. I explained where I'd been and he translated the information for my landlady who tightened her lips and shook her head before letting loose a stream of comment. It was to the effect that perhaps only when the Baroness died would 'the powers' forgive her. Allan translated 'the powers' as 'the establishment' but what Fru Rasmussen had in mind was the strange oligarchy in her country which – astonishing as it may seem to us – includes the arts and sciences as well as property and politics. They consider themselves more noble than the royal family. These powers, I knew, had denied Karen Blixen the Nobel prize for literature because she made her name writing in English. She did it with *Seven Gothic Tales*. The success of that book showed how fallible the powers had been in failing to recognise her talent during all the years in which she'd written Danish. They could not forgive her their own neglect. And her peers could not forgive *them*. When Hemingway was receiving his Nobel prize, he stated – with unsettling generosity and grace – that it should have gone to Karen Blixen instead.

But now Fru Rasmussen was telling Allan something else. He leaned forward with great attention then turned to me with a look of wonder. He'd just discovered that the unloaded boat on which he and Donal had escaped from Kiel was owned by Fru Rasmussen's late husband. All

174

three of us fell to silence and coffee-sipping while this final coincidence marked out its ground in our minds. Later there were additional facts supplied by the widow. After the war it was 'the powers' who'd broken Herr Rasmussen and deprived his business of work so that he died bankrupt. According to Allan she dealt with their vindictiveness at some length. She did not give their reasons, but these were plain to both of us. Herr Rasmussen had been a collaborator with the Nazis. He owned a small fleet of boats and they'd paid him to transport the slave labour from Copenhagen to Kiel.

When the Scotsman had gone I lay on my bed and tried to reconcile all the elements of betrayal, nationalism and revenge which would link the characters in the story I'd envisaged. Somewhat crassly, I decided I would leave out the most recent coincidence. And it seemed wise to leave out yet another, more tenuous cross-connection. That, in 1933, when Allan Chalmers sold his work to Germany, Karen Blixen was selling her work to England. And that, more than thirty-five years later, both were still considered traitors.

Gradually, the winter abated. But I was glad to note that, even in winter, Copenhagen is beautiful. The snow on the red-tile roofs, or moulding one side of the green domes and spires, served only to make them more colourful. When the mechanical sweepers cleared an open square paved with a fan-pattern of red brick, the lines of snow remaining in the crevasses made it look as though a huge and intricate lace shawl had been thrown upon the ground. The pale yellow stucco walls and the gilding on wrought iron were enhanced by snow. It provided more than an increase of light; it increased the lightness. At the height of summer the city seems airy enough, but in winter the feeling increases to a state of levitation. Walking along by the dam on my way to the studio, I regretted that my job was coming to an end. And there was the added sadness that the woman who'd brought me there was still in hospital and either unable or unwilling to see me.

There were some heartening signs, though, as that spring approached. Allan Chalmers had given up the pretence that he came to the flat in order to see me. Before long it was clear he came to see Fru Rasmussen. His learning that she was the widow of a traitor seemed to make all the difference in his attitude towards her. Of course she was an attractive and amiable woman even at first acquaintance, but the fact that she was something of a renegade who looked upon the past without dismay made him feel at ease in her company.

The feeling was mutual for, no doubt, he had told her of his war record and she saw in him the prospect for stability which had been lacking since her husband died. Soon I was excluded from the conversation with its tiresome translations. They just talked to each other – and laughed a great deal. And Allan's appearance improved quite remarkably. It was not just that he smartened his clothes; his demeanour and bearing changed. On one or two occasions when I passed the living room, and he was there with Fru Rasmussen, I noted the assurance of his gestures as he spoke fluently in a foreign language. Divorced from his native accent, this was a sophisticated middle-aged European gentleman beside whom I was gauche and, necessarily, tongue-tied. They went out quite a lot together, and only then did I realise how rarely my landlady had gone out for the evening before she met Allan. Put simply, her husband's disgrace had robbed her of friends of her own age. Even her husband's mother had fled to Italy. But now my hostess had found a partner with whom she could meet the stares and brave the whispers.

The question which was put to me in various guises soon afterwards was to determine exactly when I'd be moving out. There seemed little doubt that Allan would be moving in. When I questioned him directly on the point he was, as always, direct. Yes, they intended that he should live in the flat. I surely didn't expect him to spend the rest of his life in a hostel. He would live as Fru Rasmussen's guest until her mother-in-law died. Upon that event – which couldn't be far distant – Fru Rasmussen would either be comfortably off and free of obligations, or no worse off and free of obligations. In either case they would marry.

All this was cheering news and I congratulated myself on being the agent who had brought them together. If I hadn't enabled Donal to desert, both men would still be trapped in the hostel and Allan would never have come to the flat. Everything had worked out remarkably well. However, it did not fit the story I was writing. For one thing, reality was relying much more on coincidence than fiction would entertain. And for another the long exile of Allan Chalmers looked set for a happy ending. I was young enough at the time to be certain that if you want to convey reality it must always be sad or inconclusive or – if you wanted to reach the 'quality market' – both. Consequently, I ended the piece when Donal left on the train for home and the bitter figure of Allan Chalmers shuffled across Bernstorffsgade to the locked gates of the Tivoli Gardens. It was a scene which editors of the quality market will instantly recognise as Truth.

Now that I'm much older, and telling the story once more, I'm wary enough to realise that the reader is not a fool. The reader will know that Karen Blixen did not die in the 1958-59 winter. She died in 1962 after a triumphant tour of the United States. It became almost a royal progress during which she was acclaimed and applauded and, in a blaze of publicity, taken to the heart of that most generous nation. Her book, *Out of Africa*, climbed into the best-seller lists again – more than twenty years after it was first published.

All of that was unguessed at by her and undreamed of by me when I went back to Rungstedlund that winter. I had not seen her in hospital and one day was told that she'd insisted on going home. The doctors thought it dangerous but the Baroness always had a mind of her own, even when her body had melted to virtually nothing. She wanted to see her friends again and in circumstances where she could arrange her costume, her make-up, the lighting and her entrance. It was a measure of an unquenchable spirit that a woman of seventy-five, grievously emaciated by syphilis, should still care about such things.

I took with me a copy of the story which now had the title 'The U-Boats of Kiel'. It was a bright, crisp morning and along the stretches of the railway which came close to the Sound I could see the coast of Sweden. Not even Clara Svendsen was going to stop me this time. But as the train neared Rungsted, the apprehension grew that already I was too late. There had been no announcement of her death in the papers that morning. But what if her illness had impaired her memory and she could not recall who I was? Would she still read what I had written? Finally, even if she could remember me and did read what I offered – what if she did not *like* the story? All these doubts went chasing around my mind in a tail-snapping circle, and when eventually I walked up to the house it was with great trepidation.

Having admitted me, the maid consulted Clara Svendsen and, after only token opposition, Clara went to tell the Baroness I was there. With my hands clenched guiltily at my sides and the folded manuscript poking eloquently from my side pocket I stared at the arrangement of Masai spears on the far wall. After a few moments, Clara beckoned me from the doorway of the morning room and I went in.

Karen Blixen was seated in her wheel-chair and framed by the window. She immediately apologised that she'd not been able to see me when I'd called before. I moved closer and sat down. It was impossible to believe that anyone who looked so frail could still be alive. She was swathed in the folds of a wool poncho and her heavily jewelled fingers rested as light as snowflakes on the arms of the chair. Her head was wrapped in that curious turban arrangement she'd made her own, which seemed to accentuate the fragility of her face. But her eyes were huge and lustrous as ever. After an exchange of polite remarks she asked me how my work for the Institute was progressing.

'Very well. Drama certainly makes everything a lot clearer.'

'That is because drama exists for the moment it happens. If only people realised it, they are supporting existentialism every time they buy a ticket for the theatre.'

178

I laughed and she inclined her head to acknowledge my appreciation of the point. She went on, 'And if only poor Søren had spent more time at the play.'

This surprised me. 'Did Kierkegaard enjoy the theatre?'

'Oh, yes! He was a drama critic, you know. An excellent drama critic.' There was a pause while I assimilated this astonishing fact and before the Baroness alluded again to my earlier visit. 'I believe you told Clara you had a letter from Scheherazade!'

Somewhat embarrassed, I nodded.

She smiled. 'That was very gallant. And apt, I suppose. The doctors wonder how I've been able to cheat death so many times. Maybe it's because there is always a story to tell – and I insist on telling it.'

These remarks, I knew, were designed for me to get to the point. She could see the manuscript poking out of my pocket and must have been growing impatient. 'I've written another story,' I said.

'What is it about?'

An obligatory but always unsettling question. After a brief silence I suggested, 'It's about mercenaries, I think. Yes, mercenaries that you wouldn't allow to escape.'

The angle of her head altered perceptibly. 'Really! *I* would not! Why wouldn't I?'

'Because they had no right to freedom,' I boldly stated. From her voice and expression I knew she was intrigued. This was just the kind of veiled puzzle she enjoyed setting up in her own stories.

The Baroness parried, 'Do you mean, they absolutely did not deserve freedom, or *I* thought they did not deserve it?'

'*You* decided they shouldn't escape.'

She nodded as though accepting the blame. 'Escape into Sweden, presumably. What were they escaping from?'

'The only employer who'd ever paid them a living wage.'

After a moment's thought she remarked, 'They were very foolish mercenaries if all they asked was a living wage.'

There was no denying that. 'Yes. I suppose so. But there was a lot of competition at the time.'

'Let me read this story,' she demanded, and extended her hand.

I stood up and gave it to her. 'I'd be very grateful if you would; whenever it's convenient.'

'I shall read it now,' she said, and indicated that I should sit down again and await the verdict.

'It's a great relief that you've recovered. I was sure you were going to die.'

She glanced up from my manuscript and the intention of a smile struggled with the loose skin of her cheeks. 'Oh, I *shall* die,' she said. 'Perhaps, soon.' The smile won. 'But I shall live today.'